I0745745

Wicked Garden

LORELEI JAMES

Wicked Garden

Ridgeview Publishing

ISBN: 978-1-941869-96-3

This book is a work of fiction. All names, places and situations in this book are the products of the author's imagination. Any resemblance to actual events, locales or persons is coincidental.

The following story contains mature themes, strong language, and explicit sexual situations. It is intended for adult readers only.

Cover Design by: Meredith Blair – www.authorsangels.com
Cover Photo by: RenataAp – Bigstock.com
Interior Designed and Formatted by: BB eBooks Co., Ltd. –
www.bbebooksthailand.com

Chapter One

EDEN LaCroix embodied sin. Wicked, sinful pleasures of the flesh that'd lead a monk straight into temptation.

Billy Buchanan never claimed to be a monk, but how on earth had he ever walked away from her?

Walked? Nice try, man. You ran *away from her.*

He traced her outline on the glass partition separating them—slumberous hazel eyes, full lips, auburn curls—and was surprised his fingers didn't come away scorched.

Eden's spine straightened. Before she turned and caught him gawking, Billy stepped from view.

Way to act like a stalker, Buchanan. Real professional.

Minutes later, her secretary found him calmly leaning against the wall in the reception area. However, calm was the last thing he felt when faced with the pleasures of Eden.

"Ms. LaCroix will see you now."

Billy's knees were knocking as loud as his heart when he finally opened her office door.

"FINANCIALLY UNFEASIBLE MY ass," Eden muttered. Not every decision had to be about money.

She didn't glance up from the spreadsheet when the door clicked open. Dammit. She wasn't ready to listen to another "expert" regurgitate the same gloomy diagnosis: the building housing the community center couldn't be salvaged. "Hang on. I'll be right with you."

"No hurry. We've got all the time in the world."

A chill skittered up her spine. She'd heard those exact words before. In that low timbre, with that playful tone. Nah. Couldn't be. Her ears were playing tricks on her.

Weren't they?

Curiosity won out. Eden shoved the papers aside and looked across the desk. But the man's zipper—not his face—was at her eye-level. Before she could discern whether he dressed left or right, her gaze traveled up the charcoal-colored suit pants, past a narrow waist and broad chest covered with a crisp white dress shirt. Wide shoulders. Strong neck. Square jaw. Big grin.

A familiar big grin.

Eden's stomach knotted. "Say it ain't so," she half-whispered. "Billy Buchanan?"

"In the flesh." Billy spread his arms wide before his killer smile melted away. "Eden? You look like you've seen a ghost."

"A ghost from prom past, minus the baby blue tux." She shook her head to get the blood flowing, never taking her eyes off him.

"It's been a few years," Billy said. "You look amazing. Last time I saw you—"

"—my prom dress was down around my ankles at Motel 6. I'm surprised *you* remember since the last time I saw *you*, your scrawny ass was high-tailing it out the door."

Billy allowed a sheepish shrug, which fell short of the endearing mark Eden suspected he'd been aiming for.

"Although this trip down memory lane is fascinating"—she smiled—all teeth—"I don't have time to reminisce. I have an appointment."

Without waiting for an invitation, Billy plopped into the chair, watching her with an intensity that hadn't dimmed despite the passing of a decade. "Feather Light Consulting, right?"

That stopped her cold. "How did you know?"

"Because I *am* your appointment."

Eden's pulse spiked, but she managed a droll stare. "Still the consummate bullshit artist, I see." The wheels on her office chair squeaked as she rocked back. "I'm supposed to believe *you* work for Feather Light Consulting?"

"Yep. Since yesterday afternoon." He clicked open a battered black briefcase, propping it on his lap. "Robert Light had a heart attack Saturday night." When she gasped, he said, "Bob is recovering, but it'll take time, time Feather Light doesn't have in order to meet their current client obligations. Jim White Feather brought me here from Illinois."

Her gaze narrowed. "Why you?"

"Robert gave me a great recommendation with the engineering firm I work for in Chicago. I owe him." Billy reached into his briefcase, withdrawing a manila envelope. "Luckily I'd just wrapped up a job in Calgary. With freelance status, I'm assisting on this project with Feather Light."

"Guess it is a lucky thing for Robert."

"And for you." Billy smiled, flashing a deep dimple. "Isn't it great, us working together again? Just like old times?"

"Marvelous." The last time they'd punched a communal time clock at a local floral shop, any free moment between deliveries and customers her clothing had been askew and Billy's eager body had plastered hers to the flower cooler as they'd played the FTD version of post office.

Billy merely lifted his brows at her sarcasm.

"Although I'd like to renew specific relationships"—his eyes moved from her eyes to her lips—"I'm not interested in making friends, Eden. I'm here to do a job."

Eden chalked up the fluttering in her stomach to acid reflux, not anticipation, and certainly not from his predatory once-over.

While he rummaged in his briefcase, Eden studied the changes ten years brought to Billy Buchanan. He was still undeniably sexy, and boy-next-door handsome. His hair had darkened from blond to tawny gold. His once lanky 6'3" frame had filled out impressively. She imagined a toned athlete's body under his custom tailored clothing. Yet the quick smile with deep-set dimples and his hypnotizing blue eyes remained unchanged. Blue eyes completely focused on her.

"Jesus, Eden. You take my breath away."

The heat of his gaze evaporated every bit of moisture in her mouth. Not many things threw her, but one compliment from him and she reverted to a seventeen-year-old girl; her heart raced, her face burned, her blood pumped hot.

"Sorry. I know that was out of line. Not a good way to start this."

"So how *do* we start this, Billy? Do I ask you how you've been?

Do I ask to see your credentials?" *Or do I ask why you ran out on me?*

Billy's eyes didn't waver as the locks on the briefcase clicked. "Sure. We could also discuss the weather, or whether my old boss Nathan and his wife Tate, have contributed to the population explosion in Spearfish." He angled forward, settling his elbows on the briefcase, studying her carefully. "Or, we could skip all that crap and I could tell you why I left you and your virginity intact ten years ago."

"By all means, let's revisit that stellar moment." She lifted a hand, stopping his immediate objection. "You have one minute to get whatever guilt off your chest."

"See you've still got those rough edges."

"If I recall correctly, you were one of the few people who liked that about me," she retorted sweetly.

"Truth was, I liked everything about you."

"Funny way of showing it."

"Can you blame me? You were jailbait and at twenty-two I was a little old to be deflowering virgins."

"I knew exactly how old we both were. I chose you because I trusted you with something that mattered to me." Snapping at him wouldn't change anything. She picked up a pen and drummed it against the desk blotter. "At any rate, water under the bridge. I will admit you did do me one favor by leaving." Her lips curved into a naughty smile. "Now I take my pleasure where and when *I* like."

"Got a steady boyfriend, do you?"

"Don't need one. There are plenty of motorized ways for a woman to stay satisfied that don't involve a man. So, let's cut to the chase. What do you know about this project?"

He flipped through a binder. When Billy met her gaze again, his was all business. "The city hired Feather Light Consulting to assess whether this building can be updated with minimal cost. Or—"

"—whether the city council should sign off on it so they can use the taxpayer's dollars to build a brand new facility."

"Not a big fan of city government?"

"No, which is ironic since I am a city employee." Eden pointed to the folder. "What else does that report say?"

"The other two companies hired to assess the situation filed conflicting results. The first report suggested bulldozing the property. The second claimed it'd be cheaper to make the required updates."

"Feather Light was called in as the tie-breaker?"

"Yes. Tell me why you're so adamant about keeping the community center in this location."

She paused, trying to stay professional when this was an emotional issue for her on many levels too. "When I was growing up, if I wanted to hang out with other kids, or get advice from adults who didn't see me as a pest, I could hop on my bike and be at the community center in ten minutes. This place still caters to kids like me, single-parent, mixed-race kids with little money."

Billy's eyes softened. "Is this 'save the building at all costs' a personal crusade?"

"No. This center is crucial to the community and the hundreds of kids who walk through the doors every day. The size of the building and the state-of-the-art exercise equipment won't matter because few of the kids will be able to get out to the new building on their own."

"Meaning what?"

Eden ticked the points off on her fingertips. "No bus service. Heavy traffic on the highway makes it impossible for kids to ride their bikes with any measure of safety. Too far to walk and few of them drive."

"But the proposed site is within the city limits, even if it is on the other end of town," Billy pointed out. "The city is slated to provide transportation, connection to the bike path and other city services."

She shook her head. "Look at the preliminary report again. If the council passes the ordinance, they could take up to ten years to implement final stages of the required zoning. Ten years. The city is already considering doubling the yearly membership fee even *before* committing to a multimillion-dollar building. We have a mix of income levels here, most families struggle to pay the fees now."

"The fees are a non-issue if the building is deemed unsafe."

"True. Maybe the building needs a little TLC, but there are dozens of professional contractors volunteering to make it safe."

"Why?"

"Because so many people see it like I do. This is a community center. We fulfill many needs. We have two counselors and a dozen senior citizen volunteers come in to help out with homework or just hang around to feel useful. I predict the number of kids in juvenile detention will increase dramatically, with no other outlet for their physical and emotional frustrations. Of course, the council members believe I'm exaggerating the potential problems."

"Are you?"

"No. But I am frustrated." Their eyes locked. "I'll do damn near anything to keep the center right where it is."

Billy smiled. "Prove it. Take me on a tour, Eden. I want to see the center through your eyes."

Eden's gaze raked over his clothing. "This isn't a clean, sterile office environment. People sweat here and get dirty. You aren't afraid you'll soil your snappy suit?"

Billy stood and braced his hands on her desk. "I have no problem getting down and dirty. Do you?"

"None whatsoever."

"Good. Then let's do it."

Chapter Two

TWO HOURS LATER, Eden peeled the damp silk shirt away from her overheated skin. She'd ended Billy's tour in the basement boiler room. Pipes hissed and clattered, then quieted down to the occasional rattle and wheeze.

Billy inspected every square foot of the building. He'd asked question after question, until his low, sexy voice echoed in her ears and throbbed through her bloodstream. His cool efficiency rekindled memories she'd tried to bury years ago.

Eden might've been innocent in understanding the needs and desires that fuelled an adult physical relationship, but she and Billy had clicked on an emotional level. They'd dealt with deeper issues than where to spend Saturday night. His: the lingering effects of his father's death and his need to finish college. Hers: dealing with her drunken mother, and trying to finish high school while working nearly full-time.

In truth, it'd hurt Eden far worse when he'd run out of her life without explanation, than when he'd raced out of the motel room and refused to take her virginity. She'd counted on Billy's stability, his support, his friendship.

Eden's gaze wandered to him as he dutifully made notes. His blond hair was tousled, his funky lime-green tie askew. The smart and sexy aspects of his persona hadn't changed. But he'd honed his youthful intensity to a precise edge. She wondered if he still kissed with the same fire. Did he make love with an engineer's attention to detail and single-minded absorption in the process?

What she wouldn't give for another chance to have those energies directed at her.

Before Eden considered the implications, almost as if he'd read her mind, she became his sole focus.

"Eden?" he murmured next to her ear, sending a delicious tingle down her spine. "You spaced out for a second. Where'd you go?"

A naked trip down memory lane. "Nowhere special. Why?"

He drew a fingertip down her sweat-dampened arm. "Really? Seemed special to me. Your eyes turned liquid and soft. You licked your lips." His rapid exhalations teased the nape of her neck. "What were you tasting in your daydreams?"

You. Your lips, your mouth, your skin. She stepped back and faced him, balling her hands into fists.

His gaze dropped to her breasts and the nipples poking against her translucent blouse.

Heat suffused her face. "It *is* hot in here."

"I'll say." Billy zeroed in on the bead of sweat dripping from her temple, wiping it away with a measured sweep of his thumb.

The simple touch heightened her responsiveness and again she retreated. "Have you seen enough?"

"No." Billy started toward her, an animal stalking prey.

Eden backed up until her shoulders met a low-hanging section of ductwork. "What else?"

"I have two questions." His Italian loafers bumped her sensible black pumps. They stood knee-to-knee, hip-to-hip and chest-to-chest, face-to-face, practically breathing the same air.

Could he hear the rapid beat of her heart? Sense the fervor thickening her blood? "Ask away."

"Does this old heating system keep the entire building adequately warm?"

"Yes."

"Are you seeing anyone?"

"Not really."

"Good." His notebook crashed to the floor. He slanted his mouth over hers and kissed her.

At the warm insistence of his lips, the smooth glide of his tongue, Eden gave up both the internal and external fight. She might've leapt over the professional line, but she wanted him. The hard press of his zipper against her belly showed her how badly he wanted her too.

For several glorious minutes, she reacquainted herself with Billy's exhilarating taste; his masculine flavor flowed into her mouth and her memories. His harsh breathing, her throaty moans of pleasure and the rasp of clothing were the only sounds in the humid space.

The ravenous kiss slowed. Billy murmured against her damp skin, trailing kisses down her neck to the swell of her breasts.

His fingertips swept her hair from her face, drifting down her jawline to stroke the pulse beating in her throat. He traced her collarbones to the V of her shirt, testing the weight of her breasts in his large hands; his thumbs strayed to the silk-covered nipples.

Once again heat exploded between them. Billy crushed her against the ductwork so completely she felt every twitch of his cock on her belly, every hard muscle of his body.

The clatter of pipes startled them into breaking the kiss.

Billy backed off, but his passion-darkened eyes never left hers. They stared at one another. He tenderly brushed a curl from her forehead, letting his palm linger near her temple. "Don't look for an apology. I've been wanting to do that for three hours."

"I don't want an apology. But we weren't exactly discreet. Anyone might've walked in." She sent a nervous glance over her shoulder. "I've worked to build a decent reputation—"

"I know." He cupped her chin, urging her to look at him. "I'd never do anything to jeopardize your reputation. Doesn't change the fact I want you. Damn, do I want you, Eden. In every way imaginable."

Her insides seemed to liquefy, sending a hot trickle of excitement between her legs. "Me too. But I don't want anyone to think I slept with you in order to assure Feather Light won't recommend closing the center to the city council."

Billy froze. Then he spun on his dress shoe and crossed the concrete floor halfway before pacing back. "No offense, but nothing you could do with that luscious mouth or your incredible body would affect the outcome of this survey."

"But?"

"But when we're alone can we put the business aside?"

Here was her chance to close that chapter of her life. Might be reckless, but she deserved Billy Buchanan's undivided sexual attention, if only temporarily. "How long will you be in town?"

"A week." He watched her smooth her hair, straighten her skirt and adjust her blouse. "You busy after work tonight?"

"Yes."

"How about tomorrow night?"

"No," she admitted.

He gave her a wolfish smile. "You are now."

LATER THAT AFTERNOON Billy stretched out on the tan buffalo skin sofa in Jim White Feather's office.

He scanned the bold color scheme of Jim's extensive collection of Native American art, artifacts and photographs. The room whispered power, but exuded warmth.

A row of pictures lined a rustic pine bookshelf. Jim and his wife Cindy had taken the "go forth and multiply" suggestion quite literally.

Jim set the phone down. "What are you grinnin' at?"

"The White Feather bunch." Billy faced him, surprised by the gray streaks in Jim's long black braid. "Is eight really enough to fill your house with love?"

"*Shee.* Eight is plenty, especially with one in high school and one in diapers. Our life is never dull. Which brings me to the question of the day: how did your meeting go with the always entertaining Eden LaCroix?"

"You might've warned me she's adamantly opposed to building a new community center."

"Gave you a rough time, did she?"

An image of Eden's mouth, ripe from his forceful kisses flitted through Billy's mind. "Ah, no more than I deserved."

"Our Eden certainly is a firecracker."

"*Our* Eden?" he repeated.

"Eden is practically my little sister. She and Cindy and Jon have palled around for years."

"Then why didn't you handle this project?"

"For that very reason. Look, I wasn't thrilled when Bob took this assignment. In fact, I told him I wanted nothin' to do with it because I agree with Eden's position, the community center needs to remain in its present location. That's why I brought you in on Bob's suggestion, for an unbiased assessment."

Billy realized this was his chance to tell Jim he wasn't exactly impartial where Eden was concerned. But the damning words stuck in his throat. "Don't you think *your* opinion might affect the outcome of my recommendation?"

"I hope so." Jim shifted his enormous frame back over the desk. "Bob has absolute confidence in your ability to make the best financial decision for the client."

"You don't?"

"Like you said, I'm biased. The bottom line is different in this case. Eden is the best thing that's happened to the community center since Grace Fitzgerald left. So far the city hasn't offered her the executive position if the center relocates. She'll probably hafta leave town to find a similar payin' position. I don't want that on my conscience."

"So you're putting it on mine."

"That's why I agreed to hire you on a temporary basis. You've got nothin' at stake."

Wrong. Billy stood, pacing to the windows where pine-covered hills stretched in a sea of greenish-black.

His life had been in chaos since he'd finished his last job, one spent damn near in solitary confinement in Canada. Sure, he'd made more money in one year than in the last five, but his restlessness remained after the checks sat unspent in his bank account.

During the stint in Calgary, he realized cash had to stop being the sole factor in his decision-making. He'd wrestled with the idea of tendering his resignation to the Chicago firm, amidst visions of a slower paced life, when he'd received the frantic call about Bob's heart attack. Billy was using his vacation not only to help an old friend, but to make some tough decisions regarding his future.

And his future looked endlessly bleak. On the outside it might seem he had it all—a high-rise condo, a high paying job in a prestigious company, but on the inside, he realized none of that surface stuff mattered.

At thirty-two he was damn tired of being alone. Looking again at the happy pictures in Jim's office, Billy recognized not only did his sleek black, white and chrome office in Chicago seem drab in comparison; his life was pretty colorless too.

"You okay?" Jim asked.

"Fine. I'll keep you updated. Speaking of updates…how is Bob?"

"Better. Mostly he's scared. Betty says he might finally consider partial retirement." Jim's black eyebrows pulled together. "I don't even want to think about that."

"He's what? Sixty-seven? Didn't you consider the possibility he might not want to work forever?"

"Things have been so hectic we haven't had time to consider another partner. And now Bob's heart attack put us even further behind."

"What else can I do? I'm here, you're paying me."

Jim gestured to the stack of folders on the corner of the desk. "Take your pick. Pretty simple projects, especially for a big city hotshot like you," he grinned, "but I'd appreciate you takin' a look."

"I'll get to it right away."

"Oh, and I'm givin' you a heads up my brother Jon'll be around the condo sometime in the next couple of days. He's between tour dates."

Tour dates? Billy frowned before he remembered Jim's brother played in a rock band which mixed traditional Lakota Sioux Indian folk music with ear-splitting electric guitar and drums.

"Maybe you oughta take him along next time you talk to Eden."

"Why? Think Jon can work some musical Indian magic on her?"

"He's been tryin'. Hell, he's succeeded. Eden goes out with him whenever he's in town." Jim sighed. "I keep hopin' my little bro' will wise up, marry her and settle down, because she is perfect for him. But they're both just satisfied with hookin' up."

Hooking up. A surge of jealousy rolled through him. "With the hordes of gorgeous female fans throwing themselves at Jon on a nightly basis? I don't see the Indian rock star settling down, even with a woman as enticing as Eden."

"Enticing?" Jim repeated.

The secretary buzzing Jim's intercom allowed Billy an easy out. He snagged the folders and left before he said something else he'd regret.

Chapter Three

EDEN GREETED HER charges by name during the influx of after-school kids. The hallways teemed as they raced to the gym, a hotbed of basketball games, tumbling and jump rope classes. Her grin was as wide as theirs. This was her favorite part of the day.

She ditched her heels and played a quick round of Double Dutch, then headed to the kitchen to help serve snacks. After checking on the latest arts and craft project, she verified the volunteer list for the homework help room. Tempting to blow off her remaining paperwork and immerse herself in the enthusiasm bouncing off the walls, but part of her job was to teach responsibility and shirking hers wouldn't set a good example.

In her office, Eden immediately spied the young Sioux boy sprawled in the chair across from her desk. She risked an indulgent smile. "Thomas!"

"What do you want done today? 'Cause they're lettin' me play forward later."

"I didn't see you in the cafeteria. Did you get a snack?"

He angled his Denver Nuggets baseball cap toward the carpet. His unlaced high-top tennis shoes swung beneath the chair. "Not hungry."

Thomas had more pride than the average twelve-year old. But pride didn't fill hungry, growing bellies. She unwrapped the Rice Krispie treat and set it on the edge of her desk.

"Too bad. My eyes were bigger than my stomach."

"S'pose I could eat it." He ate with a delicacy that belied his age and gender. "What'm I doin' today?"

Eden pointed to the cardboard boxes on the floor. "Those are the monthly newsletters from the last four years. I want them filed chronologically."

Panic flared in his brown eyes. "Chrono-what?"

"Chronologically. In order of date, January 1999, February 1999, and so on."

"Do I hafta *read* them?"

"Not all the way through, just enough to put them in the correct order." Thomas had let it slip he lagged behind his classmates in school. Despite his grumbling, she'd decided to challenge his mind, hoping he'd recognize mental aptitude was as important as physical skills.

"Can we at least listen to some music? Like KILI?"

KILI FM was a Native American radio station that played an odd assortment of tunes from Powwow music to rap. "Sounds good."

"Cool." He flopped on the floor behind the chair, dumping the box contents into a messy pile.

Eden turned the boom box on low and sorted through her own stacks. The rhythmic chanting and steady beat of the tom-tom drums made soothing background noise. The music reminded her of Jon White Feather, a.k.a. Johnny Feather, a drummer/singer with the Lakota musical group, Sapa, was due to roll back into town soon.

Jon personified rock star: long black hair, tribal tattoos, all buffalo-leather clothes and warrior attitude. He was a smokin' hot, sweet-talkin' Indian who could charm the panties off any woman—and probably had, but Eden didn't care. They had a great time together.

With her, Jon could just be Jon, her old college buddy, not Johnny, heartthrob to the Indian nation. With him, she could be Eden, the wicked temptress, not Eden the buttoned-up community center director. Sex was off-the-charts phenomenal between them because neither one pretended it was anything more than two old friends acting on mutual lust.

Would sex with Billy be that explosive?

Not helping you concentrate, Eden.

Twenty minutes later she hit the total button on the calculator and frowned.

"How is it possible you look beautiful even wearing a scowl?"

Billy's gravelly voice brought color to her cheeks. She glanced up—his crotch was eye-level again—and saw he wore thigh-hugging faded jeans rather than suit pants.

A boyish snort sounded from behind the chair. Thomas leapt to his feet. "Man, that was so lame."

"Thomas. Be nice."

Billy thrust his hand out. "Billy Buchanan."

Grudgingly Thomas accepted the proffered hand. "Thomas Fast Wolf. Billy, huh? Another guy by the name of Billy, *Billy Mills*, came here last year and talked to us. Ever heard of him?" Thomas recited

Billy Mills's feats of Olympic glory, while Eden stood by with her mouth hanging open. The kid did pay attention.

"I'm not much of a track and field fan, but I do like the occasional basketball game." Billy regarded Thomas's hat. "The Nuggets aren't as good as the Bulls."

Thomas snorted. "The Bulls are a has-been team."

"Better than a *wanna-be* team."

"Enough." Eden directed her attention to Thomas. "If you're finished sorting, scoot. I don't want you to miss a minute of your game. I'll see you same time next week."

"Aren't you comin' down to watch me?"

His tone was shy of pleading. Thomas, no stranger to disappointment, rarely asked anything of her. "Absolutely."

He treated Eden to a broad smile, but gave Billy a skeptical once-over. "So Mr. Bulls fan, you oughta come down and see how real basketball is played. Some of the guys in junior high are bigger than you. Bet you'd get your butt kicked."

"Thomas!"

But Billy merely shrugged. "Good thing I wore my butt-kickin' shoes. I'll be there after I have a word with Ms. LaCroix." After the door closed, he said, "Interesting kid. What's he doing in the office when he'd rather be wreaking havoc in the gym? Working off some sort of punishment?"

"No. A trade." She fixed her gaze on the calculator keys. "Thomas helps me out once a week, no big deal."

Silence stretched, long and snaky as the calculator tape.

"I see."

"What?"

"That you're paying his club fees and letting him work it off in here."

Why bother denying it? "Yes. That way he doesn't feel he's a charity case. It keeps him out of trouble."

"How many fees are you paying out of your own pocket?"

"It doesn't matter. Thomas is basically a good kid. But that'd change in a heartbeat if he didn't have anywhere to go after school. His family situation isn't the best. Sometimes he sneaks in here at night to avoid a beating. I've tried to tell him how dangerous that is but he doesn't listen and I shudder to think what'd happen to him if the center closed."

Eden squeezed her eyelids shut, remembering Thomas's resentful look turning hopeful when she'd offered him the trade. Having Thomas around was a constant reminder of how far she'd come. One person could make a difference in the lives of kids who had so little. "This place is everything to him."

Gentle fingers touched her cheek. Her eyes opened to see Billy standing within kissing distance. "Seems this place is everything to you too," he murmured, stroking the vulnerable skin by her ear.

She stepped away from his tempting touch. "Not here."

Billy's eyes clouded to murky gray. "If I had my way I'd close the blinds, lock the door, throw you across the desk and fuck you until neither of us could walk out."

The fire in his gaze rushed over her in a blast of heat.

"If I'd had my way yesterday, I would've hiked up your skirt, spread your legs wide, bent you over that duct in the basement and pounded into you until you came, screaming my name."

Eden clenched her legs together to stave off the tremors.

"Surprised?"

"Not by the visual. But I was surprised you weren't here earlier today."

"I was. The janitor let me in at six o'clock. I hung around until nine, videotaped some footage."

She frowned. "You should've told me yesterday you planned on checking out the building at the crack of dawn."

"Why does that matter?"

"Because I'd have made a point to be here to answer any of your questions."

"Or to try to steer me away from areas you don't want me to see?" he countered.

"Not true. I didn't deny you access to any area yesterday, and you damn well know it." Eden folded her arms over her chest. "I just don't like the idea of you sneaking around unsupervised."

"Need I remind you, you aren't my client and I don't answer to you?"

"As administrator of this facility, I expect you to give me advance notice on when you plan to be on site."

"Keeping tabs on me?"

"No. Like every other person who walks through those doors, when you're here, you're my responsibility. And if something should happen—"

"—like if a chunk of that water-damaged plaster ceiling on the third floor fell on me? Or if I tripped over the four-inch foundation crack in the basement and split my head open?"

"See?" Eden jabbed a finger in his sternum. "That's exactly what I mean. We haven't discussed a damn thing about any of your initial findings. I'm sure the other companies reports made you aware of the safety concerns—"

Billy pressed her palm flat to his chest. "I haven't read the other reports."

She blinked. "What?"

"I haven't looked at them. They're still in Bob's office."

"Why?"

"Because they don't matter. Those reports are their opinions, not mine. I didn't want my judgment skewed beforehand." Billy brought her wrist to his mouth, kissing the soft skin until her breath hitched. "I'm sorry. I blew it, all right? I should've informed you first. So, in the future, I'll give you a heads up before I start poking around."

"Good."

"When and where can I see you tonight?"

Eden disentangled herself and grabbed a piece of paper. "Here's my address. Come by after seven."

"I can't wait."

Chapter Four

As BILLY SPED through Eden's neighborhood, he scarcely noticed the architectural details—the Victorian painted ladies, the quaint brick bungalows or the structural designs inspired by Frank Lloyd Wright.

He parked in front of the detached garage, nearly vaulting the evergreen hedge separating the sidewalk from the driveway. After passing through the arbor twined with yellow roses, he paused at the steps. A white envelope was tacked to the front door, fluttering in the evening breeze.

Disappointment clenched his gut as he strode across the spacious porch and snatched the envelope. The note read:

Since you're so adept at sneaking around my building, you have five minutes to find me. If you succeed, you get to be in charge tonight. If you fail, be prepared to surrender to my every whim. Ring the doorbell and the timer starts.

A thrill shot through him that buttoned-up, professional Eden hadn't neglected her playful side. He set his watch, swung open the door, poked the doorbell and stepped across the threshold.

Billy's gaze darted up the staircase but he started his search in the living room. She wasn't hiding behind the velvet drapes or in the coat closet. In the dining room, the space under the antique trestle table remained empty. The mahogany china cabinet was too small to crawl inside, even for a sprite like Eden.

He dashed through the doorway to a kitchen painted in tones of lavender and purple. When he paused in front of a bright red half-bath tucked underneath the staircase, he realized Eden hadn't shed her funky bohemian side.

Damn. Two and a half minutes had passed.

Billy took the stairs at a dead run.

Upstairs he faced seven doors—all closed. The first one revealed a small linen closet. The second and third, empty bedrooms. The fourth room displayed a four-poster canopy bed and was sumptuously decorated in lace, velvet and silk.

Behind the fifth door he found a large pink and black bathroom, complete with a claw foot tub. Door number six led to an attic. Billy flicked on the light switch and barreled up the wooden stairs. Boxes covered the wide-planked floor. No Eden. He raced down the stairs.

He turned the crystal doorknob, pushed open the heavy oak door to the last room, and found Eden sprawled on a weight bench. A Stairmaster stood in one corner, a TV/DVD combo in the other. A purple yoga mat was spread on the carpet.

Somehow he ripped his gaze away from her to check the time.

Four minutes, forty-five seconds. He'd made it. His triumphant smile increased when he got his first complete look at the sexy outfit Eden was *almost* wearing. Red bustier. Red garters hooked to shimmery black stockings. Black fuck-me stilettos.

Instantly, his dick stirred to life.

Her cherry-colored mouth curved into a secretive feminine smile. "I was beginning to wonder if you'd gotten lost."

"Just losing my mind when I think of you." He stalked toward her. "You were lounging here the whole time?"

"Mmm." One finger stroked her plumped cleavage. "You cut it close." She tossed the timer to the floor. "Ten seconds left, by my calculations."

"Fifteen seconds by mine," he corrected. "But I am the winner. I can do whatever I want, right?"

"Within reason."

"I'd never do anything to hurt you when I've thought about nothing but touching you all day." Billy crouched in front of her, his hands glided up the outside of her stocking-clad legs, over lace-covered narrow hips and rib cage. His thumbs brushed the generous swell of her breasts, purposely avoiding her nipples, lingering across the graceful sweep of her collarbone. He palmed her shoulders, lightly trailing his fingers down her arms to clasp her small hands.

He tugged her to her feet, angling his head to draw in the fragrant scent of her hair. "Kiss me."

Her lips parted and she latched onto his tie, hauling his mouth to hers. Not a sweet, welcoming kiss; Eden inhaled him with a tongue thrusting, clash of lips and teeth.

A heartfelt groan had him gathering her silken hair in his fists.

Eden broke her mouth free, nibbling over his jawbone up to whisper, "The bed's in the other room."

"We don't need a bed. I want to look at you. Stand right here." Billy expected her to protest, but she placed her feet on the carpet where he'd indicated. "Beautiful. Close your eyes."

Her long lashes drifted shut.

Billy circled her, dusting his fingertips over her petal soft skin. Standing behind her, he let his breath waft across her damp nape until she shivered. "Did you wear this outfit to tease me?"

"Yes."

"Hold still while I take it off." He sank to his knees, running his palms up the back of her muscled calves, across that expanse of fabulous thigh. The gap between garter and stocking held his fascination and he bent to taste it.

Eden gasped. Her gasp morphed into a full-blown moan when his tongue licked a wet path up to the sweet curve of her hip. He explored that exquisitely sensitive skin, using feathery strokes on the outside of her legs.

"Unhook the garters," he said gruffly.

She fumbled with the stockings until they were free of the clasps.

The sight of Eden bending over, smooth ass pushed out, the line of her spine flat, made him adjust his erection. He'd take her that way, cock grinding into her sweet, hot pussy as his fingers dug into those curvy hips.

"Turn around and sit on the bench."

"Can I open my eyes?"

"Yes." Billy fell to his knees. "Let's get those sexy shoes off."

She lifted her leg, placing the toe of her black pump on his shoulder. Cupping her ankle, he removed her shoe and slid off the stocking, licking, nibbling and kissing each portion of newly bared skin. He repeated the agonizingly slow process on the other leg. Once finished, he scrutinized her, noting her ragged breathing as he placed his hands on her knees.

He tugged at the bustier. "Take it off."

"The zipper is in the back, so if you're expecting a sexy strip-tease—"

Billy blocked her dissent with his mouth. He fed on her sweetness, groaning at the press of her lace-covered breasts to his chest. He hungered for this hot-blooded woman moaning in his arms and wouldn't be satisfied until he memorized the distinctive taste of her as she climaxed against his tongue.

Reaching behind her, he yanked on the zipper. The bodice fell and he tossed it aside. He blazed a trail of wet, hot kisses to the tops of her breasts.

"These are perfect. I want to take hours learning how you like to be touched here. But for now…" He sucked as much of that soft flesh into his mouth as he possibly could. Feasting on her breasts until the pink tips bloomed a darker rose.

She cried out, arching her back, straining against him.

His cock swelled from her throaty growls. He leapt to his feet and eased her back onto the inclined bench seat.

Billy unknotted the tie and threw it behind him. He made short work of his dress shirt, shoes and socks. He only unbuttoned the top button of his slacks. Again he slipped his hands up her body, savoring every sexy inch. "What's really going through that sharp mind, gorgeous?"

Her eyes turned liquid, a soft hue that bespoke of raw passion. "I've thought of this since I was seventeen."

"Tell me what you want."

"I want you to put your mouth on me."

Smiling, he bent and kissed her knee.

"Smart-ass," she hissed.

"You weren't very explicit."

She propped herself up on her elbows, eyes gleaming. "I want your mouth sucking between my legs until I come."

He stared at her and grinned. "That's the hottest thing I've ever heard."

"And I want it right now."

He hooked his fingers inside her red lace panties, dragging them down her long legs and carelessly tossed them over his shoulder. "You asked for it. Remember that when you're begging me to let you come."

Chapter Five

"I CAN TAKE it," Eden said boldly, even when the sparkle in his eye sent shivers to her core.

Billy gently nudged her and she lowered her back flat, staring at the ivory ceiling. Perched on the end of the weight bench, he placed his hands on her knees. "Wider. Show me what I've won. Show me what's mine tonight."

A wave of desire washed over her. She stretched her legs, letting her heels rest on the metal rungs of the bench. Her eyes closed when his hot flesh moved into the space she'd created between her thighs.

His finger slid through the wetness of her pussy, stopping to trace the triangle of curls. "So pretty. So pink." One hand stroked her thigh. His mouth came into play, kissing her hipbones, the sensitive line of skin below her navel. A warm tongue skated across each rib as he made a thorough journey up her body.

His thumb flicked across that pouting bundle of nerves at her center, gliding down to rest in her slick opening. He repeated the path up and down her wet slit, gradually increasing the rhythm so it was a constant stroking.

Eden began to thrash. Even the fake leather bench seat was too much stimulus on her skin. She wanted his mouth everywhere—on her lips, on her breasts, on her aching sex. Finally that wayward mouth reached her nipples, using the tiniest amount of tongue on tips. "Please, Billy."

As he latched onto her nipple with his teeth, he slid two fingers deep inside her pussy.

The sensation of his hungry mouth suckling her breast, his long fingers pumping in and out, his thumb rubbing her clit, sent her careening into space. She pressed up to meet his demanding fingers, clutching his strong shoulders, shudders racking her from scalp to toes as he milked even the tiniest spasm.

After her sex quit pulsing, Eden opened her eyes, mortified by being so quick on the trigger.

But Billy's intense gaze indicated he hadn't minded her speedy trip to climax. His hand slid from between her thighs, smoothed a wet line up her belly, which he followed with this tongue. "Beautiful," he growled against her flushed skin.

Eden dove her hands into his thick hair. Her impatient palms tracked the iron contours of his broad shoulders, down his powerfully muscled back. She tugged at the wool fabric of his suit pants. "I want you," she murmured against his mouth.

"No." Billy pressed into a push-up position, using the bar above her head as leverage. "I want to look in your eyes when I make you come this time." With that declaration, he stepped back, circled her ankles and planted her feet on his shoulders.

She struggled to sit up. "What are you doing?"

"Putting my mouth on you." His tongue swirled a path up the

inside of her thigh. "Stay like that," he warned, "watch me taste you."

"B-but, it's too soon, I-I can't possibly—"

"You can," he said, licking a wide swath over the center of her, "you will." His thumbs spread her folds apart, dragging his mouth up and down the dripping furrow. In a breathless second, he jammed his hot, wiggling tongue inside her pussy as high as it would reach.

"Oh. My. God." The muscles below her belly button rippled as his mouth worked magic. Soft hair brushed the inside of her thighs making them tremble anew.

"Jesus, you taste like some dark exotic fruit," he groaned, lapping at the moisture pouring from her sex. Billy's head lifted, his mouth glistened with her juices. "Keep your eyes on mine." Again his nimble tongue connected with her clit, drawing a series of figure eights.

Blood rushed to the swollen membranes as that elusive point pulsed. The steel bar dug into her lower back as her legs tensed, her nipples beaded, a zing of white-hot heat shot straight to her core.

When the vibrations started, Billy trained his eyes on her face, and his callused fingers tweaked her nipple.

Eden moaned as orgasm number two flooded her. She watched Billy's heavy-lidded eyes as the climax he'd wrought emblazoned a mark on her.

The delicious throbbing slowed. Stopped. He scattered kisses along the tops of her thighs. Replete, she flopped back on the hard bench with a gusty sigh.

Billy's mouth meandered up her torso, tasting the dips and valleys of her sated flesh until he reached her lips. His gentle breath swept her mouth open and his tongue plunged inside, sharing his heat and her musky tang. He lifted her from the bench and settled her on the yoga mat.

Eden stretched, coiling around him with the languor of a sun-warmed snake. After endless, glorious minutes of Billy's loving caresses and reverent touches, he pulled away. She opened her eyes lazily. "What?"

"You are amazing."

"But I haven't done anything besides let you have your wicked way with me."

Smiling, he twined a damp curl around his finger. "Would you believe me if I said that *was* my biggest fantasy?"

"No." To prove her point, she slid a bare thigh up his leg until it connected with the hard ridge of his erection. "I'd say my biggest fantasy involves ripping those pants to shreds." She reached for the zipper, but he blocked her move. A warning flashed in the back of her mind.

"Before you scorch my hair with that dirty look, I'm not going anywhere." Billy pinned her arms above her head. "Leave them there."

"Why?"

"Because you haven't called mercy yet." His wicked mouth wended between her aching breasts. He lapped at the generous curves until she writhed beneath him. He coated his middle finger with her juices, slipping it down to rest on the rosy bloom of her anus.

She froze, half in fear, half in excitement, automatically contracting that muscle.

"Has any man ever fucked you here?"

"No."

He looked her square in the eye, his questing finger stayed in place. "Since I blew taking your virginity ten years ago, will you let me take this one? Let me be the first man to put my cock in your ass?"

Eden's mouth went as dry as the Badlands. She'd been curious about that particular act, but hadn't trusted other lovers to initiate her into the dark pleasure of anal sex. But Billy had figured out her secret desire and offered to make it come true.

She nodded.

Billy growled, clamped his lips to hers, snaring her attention in a drawn out, tongue numbing kiss. Her body arched closer to his, lost in passion flaring between them.

When he finally, slowly breached that untried area, the sensation was so acute she gasped in his mouth.

He steadily pumped his finger, and slid his thumb into her slit, wiggling it inside her. "Tighten your pussy muscles. Now."

Right when Eden squeezed, Billy pressed his thumb and his middle finger together, so she felt him stroking both walls.

"Oh. My. God."

"Wild, huh?"

"Yeah. Is that sort of what it'd feel like to have…"

His eyes glittered. "Tell me. To have what?"

"To be filled in both places at one time."

"Would you like to try that? Have a cock in your cunt and another one in your ass? At the same time?"

"Uh. Yeah."

"Real? Or a facsimile?"

"Both."

Billy kissed her, not a hard punishing kiss, but softly. Sweetly. He whispered, "Where is your vibrator?"

She went utterly still. "W-w-what?"

"Your vibrator." His hand slipped over her sweat-slickened belly to the thatch of curls and stroked her clit. "Don't play coy. You told me you don't need a man to take your own pleasure. Tell me where it is."

It was hard to create a plausible lie when he used such sublime diversions. "Umm…What are you going to do with it?"

"I won't use it for double penetration right now."

Her brain stuck on *right now*. "Oh." Eden swallowed hard. "What do you have planned?"

Billy's low chuckle rumbled against her breast. "Guess you'll have to trust me to find out." He lifted his head a fraction. "Do you trust me, Eden?"

"I-I—"

His pink tongue lapped shiny wet circles around her equally pink nipple. His cool breath drifted across the moistened tip and she gasped when his demanding fingers began plucking her other nipple. "Where is it?"

"Bottom drawer in the bureau in my room," she blurted.

He grinned, raced out and was back in the room with the buzzing purple rubber vibrator before she felt the sting of embarrassment. "Billy, it's not what you think—"

"No? I think you're sexy." The vibrating tip teased her puckered nipples. "I think you should relax and enjoy this." He drew circles around her breasts, zigzagging the buzzing wand down the length of her torso. "I sure as hell am."

Billy nipped love bites along her hips. He slipped the pointed end over her clit and held it there. "Like that?" he murmured, watching every pleasurable twitch of her body.

Eden's breath caught. "Too intense. Move it down."

The rubber shaft slipped through the wetness between her thighs, creating pulsating warmth. He traced the mouth of her sex, dipping down to press the tip into the strip of skin separating her two openings. She tensed, half-afraid, half hoping he'd just dive right in to the naughty temptation.

But he moved the vibrator up to the wet furrow of her pussy and pushed it in.

Her mouth opened in a cry of delight, which he seized with a bruising kiss. He rocked the buzzing shaft in and out. With his hard cock grinding into her hip and his lips controlling hers, she wanted to wallow in the feeling of utter wantonness.

Instead, she exploded, gasping as shards of pleasure erupted. Heart racing, sweat dripping, pelvis pumping, she thrashed against the sticky mat as the most intense orgasm of her life nearly knocked her unconscious.

At one point Eden was vaguely aware of Billy removing the vibrator and whispering soothing words, gifting her with tender kisses, prolonged caresses. He enfolded her in his arms, and whisked her off to her bed. Cool cotton sheets brushed her skin, then his firm body nestled against hers beneath the comforter.

She closed her eyes. "Let me catch my breath, then it'll be your turn."

"No hurry." His warm breath ruffled the hair on the back of her head. "We've got all the time in the world."

Content, she snuggled into Billy's embrace.

And fell fast asleep.

EDEN WOKE UP naked and alone, darkness shadowing her room. She called out a tentative, "Billy?"

No answer. Not that she blamed him for taking off.

She flipped the covers and shivered. Donning her chenille robe, she tiptoed into the hallway. The Tiffany-style lamp threw a pattern of rainbow colors against the wall. She double-checked the doors downstairs, but Billy had locked them before leaving. Still, she felt every bit a selfish idiot. What'd possessed her to fall asleep?

When she'd crawled back into her bed and turned on the night-light, she noticed the sheet of paper perched on the adjoining pillow. She grinned. Cocky man. He'd used her vibrator as a paperweight. The note read:

Eden,

I didn't have the heart to wake you. Late lunch tomorrow? You pick the place.

Billy

PS-Tomorrow it's your turn

She clasped the letter to her breast. He wasn't upset? How had she forgotten his innate sweetness? Right. She'd been so bowled over by his sexpertise; she'd forgotten Billy Buchanan was comprised of more qualities than talented fingers and a skillful mouth. Smiling, she switched off the light and returned to sleep.

Chapter Six

"MR. BUCHANAN IS here," Shelby announced through the intercom early the next afternoon.

Eden's pulse spiked. She peered at the clock. Late lunch meant little interruption for the surprise she'd planned. She fluffed up her hair and smoothed the crease from her black linen mini-skirt. "Send him in."

The door swung open, but Billy's handsome face was hidden behind a camcorder. He kept the camera trained on her as he folded his solid frame into the chair opposite her desk. "Today we're in the office of Eden LaCroix, administrator for the Spearfish Community Center. Ms. LaCroix, I'd like to record your opinions on the future of this facility."

"What is this?"

Billy depressed a button and rested the compact machine on his knee. "I told you I tape footage for every project."

"Why?"

"Easier to find problems in case I missed something pertinent the first time around."

"Does that happen often? You miss something important?"

He frowned and fiddled with the angle of the LCD screen. "Sometimes when I least expect it."

"And if I refuse?"

His eyes met hers in challenge. "I'll use my toy on someone else."

Hoo-boy. Her body heated, remembering his proficiency with *toys* last night. "Fine. Let's get started. Don't forget we have a lunch date and I'm starved."

AS BILLY TRAINED his camera on Eden, he felt like he'd been split in two. The professional half calmly asked questions and appeared in perfect control. The testosterone-laden half gloated at the shine in Eden's eyes, the high color in her cheeks, the way the lens caught every beautiful nuance of her face.

Had his attention to her sexual pleasure last night put the extra glow in her today? Nah. He couldn't take credit. Eden was smart, striking, determined and it showed in person as well as on tape.

He listened as Eden rattled off the comprehensive history of the community center. She presented him a detailed list on how the city could improve and promote the community center in its present location. Some of her suggestions were unfeasible, but the majority of the ideas were reasonable.

Billy kept his questions to a minimum and let Eden's passion for the project speak for itself. "That should be enough for now," he said, powering down the unit and shoving it in the carrying case.

Eden rounded the desk, cocking a slim hip on the corner. Her short skirt rose up, showcasing an extra inch of marvelous thigh. Automatically his attention traveled higher. She rolled her shoulders back, the buttons on the sleeveless cinnamon-colored blouse stretched, exposing a creamy line of breast encased in a lacy peach bra.

Billy's hungry gaze met her impish glimmer.

"Seen enough?" she murmured throatily.

"Not nearly." He stood and pressed closer, letting her knee brush the bulge beneath his fly. "I wish I'd had this camera last night."

"Sorry I conked out."

Billy slid a quick glance to the closed metal blinds separating her office from the reception area. "I want to kiss you," he said, leaning close enough to taste her sweet breath. "I need to feel your mouth on mine so I know last night wasn't another elaborate fantasy I'd conjured up when I'm alone in my bed thinking about you."

"You've been thinking about me?"

"For years." Before he could erase those scant inches and fasten his mouth to hers, Eden ducked under his arm.

"If you've waited that long then another few hours won't matter. You're not kissing me in here." She snagged an oversized purse. "But if you're really good, I might give you a kiss in the car on the way to lunch." Her amused eyes zeroed in on the swelling beneath his zipper. "Probably won't happen though, because we both know how much you enjoy being bad."

Billy's response, "I'll be good, I promise," fell on deaf ears as she sailed out the door.

SHE'D CHOSEN AN upscale Italian restaurant in a renovated turn-of-the-century warehouse showcasing exposed maroon bricks, metal beamed ceilings, original wide-planked wooden flooring with deeply weathered grooves. The structure appealed to him on a professional level. Add in old-fashioned gas lamps updated with electricity, crisp ivory linen tablecloths, pots of fresh herbs and private high-backed booths and it was charmingly romantic.

The college-aged male waiter recited the lunch specials, warning them the kitchen was about to close. After ordering, Billy noticed Eden's fingers nervously plucking the tablecloth.

"What's wrong?"

"Nothing. It's just weird, us having lunch together."

"Because we're in public?" Anyone strolling by had to look damn hard to see them, as they'd chosen a secluded booth away from the kitchen and the front door.

"No. Because when we were younger neither of us had enough money to eat someplace this nice. And we'd rather have been…"

Billy twined her fidgety fingers through his. "We'd rather have been making out like crazy, all hot mouths, frenzied hands and unfulfilled aches."

Color rose on her cheekbones. "Like last night?"

"Regrets?"

"None. Except for me falling asleep. I'm really sorry."

"Don't be. I told you. Last night was for you." He grinned. "I'm not worried. I'll get mine."

Eden grinned back, a bit smugly, in his opinion. "Sooner than you might think." She deflected his next question by pointing to his briefcase. "Is this a business lunch?"

"No. But it'd appear that way to anyone who might see us eating together."

"Good thinking." She settled into the cushioned leather backrest. "So, with all the stuff going on at the center, you haven't told me about your fabulous life in Chicago."

Fabulous. What a laugh. "What do you want to know?"

"The usual. Do you go to Bulls games? Do you walk along the waterfront?" She brushed a lock of hair from her forehead. "Do you and your friends heckle the hapless Cubs? Or do you prefer fine dining when you're out on the town?"

"Sometimes I do those things. I've also been known to wolf down a Chicago style pizza and a hot dog or two. But mostly, I work, so my social life is pretty pathetic. Plus, I've been in Canada for the last eighteen months working on an intensive restoration."

"Eighteen months? Isn't that a long time to be away from home?"

Funny, he'd never considered his condo home; he was so rarely there. He spent more time in his battered office chair than on his brand new living room couch. "I'm used to it. The majority of my projects are done in other cities."

"Bet you've been some pretty cool places?"

"I guess. What about you?"

"Me? I've never ventured from here. Spearfish has always felt like home." Frowning, she stirred her tea. "But now with the future of the community center up in the air, it's a little scary wondering where I'll end up."

An awkward silence lingered until the waiter interrupted with their salads. Billy was determined to get the conversation back on personal ground. "I love the Black Hills. Now if I can only convince my baby sister Maggie to stick around here."

Eden's fork stopped midway to her mouth. "You have a sister who lives here?"

"Maggie lives in Rapid City. She signed on as a civilian computer programmer at Ellsworth Air Force Base a few months back. I hadn't been able to visit her until the job in Calgary ended."

"You planned on coming back to South Dakota *before* Jim called you?"

Here was the moment of truth. Billy fixed his gaze to hers so there'd be no misunderstanding. "Yes. Bob's heart attack just speeded up the process. I'd intended to spend time in Spearfish long before that."

"Did you know… Never mind. Don't answer."

"Yes. I knew you still lived here."

She rooted around in her salad. "Why didn't I know you had a sister?"

"Actually, I have two sisters. Lacy is married with two kids and works as a publicist in New York City." He focused on the muted fresco covering the far wall. "I didn't tell you about my family because my senior college year wasn't an easy time for me. My mother went off the deep end after my dad's death. Luckily, Lacy had escaped to NYU. I'd ended up here on a full scholarship and lived with my grandma, but poor Maggie was stuck with our mom."

He remembered the guilt, the hysterical, late-night phone calls from his frightened sister. His sister who was the same age as Eden. Talk about a wakeup call. The night when Eden doffed her dress in the motel room and stood in front of him completely naked? As much as Billy wanted her, his brain got stuck on whether his little sister was losing her virginity to a lecherous college boy in a sleazy motel after her senior prom.

That idea literally deflated his plans and he was too embarrassed to tell Eden the truth. Instead, he'd yanked his pants up over his limp cock and vanished into the night.

The next week college finals had started. After the last stunt his mother pulled, he'd had no choice but to leave right after exams, skipping his college graduation ceremony. As soon as he'd settled Maggie in New York with Lacy, he'd joined the Chicago firm.

A warm, soft hand covered his. "I'm sorry. Guess I was so self-absorbed back then I didn't see you suffered with your own family problems."

"Not self-absorbed, Eden. Self-conscious, maybe. Self-reliant, definitely. But you are the least self-centered person I've ever known."

The meals arrived and they ate in companionable silence. Eden sucked a fat piece of shrimp from her fork, releasing the tines a millimeter at a time, swallowing with gusto and then licked her lips.

An image flashed of her wrapping those shiny red lips around his cock. Sucking frantically and her beautiful throat muscles working as she swallowed. The urge surfaced to sweep everything from the table, spread her wide and fuck her fast and furiously on top of it.

The air thickened and the booth seemed to close in.

When the waiter appeared to clear plates and detailed the dessert menu, Eden fished around in her purse, pulled out a twenty and handed it to him. "Nothing else. We won't have to bug you and we can get on with our business."

Before Billy considered Eden's motives, she'd squeezed next to him in his side of the booth, her right thigh pressed to his left. Her body heat seared him and her heady, dark scent made his already shallow breathing more difficult.

"Put your briefcase on the table and open it, so it looks like we're working."

A tiny kernel of anxiety unfurled in his gut, but he placed his briefcase on the middle of the table and popped the locks. "Are we working?" he asked inanely, removing file folders.

"Not you." Eden's cool mouth suctioned to the hot skin below his ear. He shuddered at the simple touch. Her left hand arced down the center of his body from the knot in his tie to the buckle on his pants. "However, I have catch-up work to do. It is my turn, remember?"

The full impact of her words sunk in when she unbuckled his belt. "Eden—"

"Billy," she whispered back in a mocking tone, making quick work of his zipper. "I'm going to stroke your cock right here under the table until you explode in my hand. And you're going to let me."

Turned on beyond measure, he said not a word.

"Sit back and open your legs wider." Eden's exhalations tickled his neck. "Pretend you're studying a market analysis." Her fingers slipped into the gap in his boxers. When the warmth of her hand circled his aching cock, Billy groaned.

She stroked from root to tip, letting the plump head rub against the hard ridge of her palm. Drops of pre-come dribbled down, making the glide of her hand easier, increasing the sensations until his buttocks tightened and the vein running up his cock began to pulse.

If anyone passed their table, all they'd see was two heads bent close, engrossed in the sheaf of papers on the table between them.

Eden repeated the words he'd said last night. "Tell me what you want."

"I want to fuck you. Hard. Fast. Right now." His hand moved under the table and he tried to stop her activity on his dick. "Let's go."

"No. You let go." She nipped his earlobe, knocking his hand away with her knee. "My turn to call the shots." She stopped the slide of her hands to feather butterfly touches from his balls to the weeping tip. "You're so damn sexy, Billy. I want to feel you come. I won't stop until you do."

As he nuzzled Eden's soft hair, his tension slipped away. No doubt if he would've slid his hand under her skirt, he'd have expected her compliance. Hell, he was a modern man, equal time and all that. He admitted it felt good to let Eden be in charge. And if the euphoric look on her face was any indication, she was getting off on the naughty exhibition as much as he was.

"I wish it was my mouth on you." She squeezed from the bottom of his shaft up, her fingers a tight ring as she rubbed her thumb over the slick tip. "My lips, teeth and tongue. I'd get your cock really wet. See if I could deep throat you. Then when you were teetering on the edge, I'd suck you dry and swallow every drop."

"Enough. God, I can only take so much." Damn. He was close. Too close, but he had no intention of trying to hold back.

"Do you like me talking dirty? You'll like it even better when I do this." She increased her strokes.

The muscles in his groin tightened, his balls drew taut. Helplessly he gathered the linen tablecloth in his fist. He focused on a rainbow glimmer of crystal reflecting on the table as his rigid sex pulsed toward completion. A white-hot flame shot out of the end of his cock, his head fell back and he groaned long and low as his seed flooded her hand.

A tender kiss brushed his lips, followed by a soft cloth on his crotch wiping away the remnants of his explosion.

Billy slowly cracked his eyelids, half-afraid he'd been dreaming again and he'd wake to nondescript walls of another hotel room with his dick clutched in his own hand.

But his eyes met Eden's and clashed in a heated frenzy of desire. She lifted her hand and wickedly licked the tips of her fingers.

A possessive need ignited his blood.

Billy tucked himself in and zipped up. Briefcase closed, he hauled Eden from the booth, out the door and into his car.

His hands clutched the steering wheel. He didn't utter a peep after his Neanderthal tactic of practically dragging her by the hair from the restaurant. He didn't dare touch her; once he started he wouldn't stop. When he finally screeched to a halt outside the condo, he faced her.

"Look. I didn't mean to make you mad."

"I'm not mad."

"Why were you in such a hurry to get away?"

Billy's hands shook when he reached for her. Somehow he kept his touch gentle as he traced her baby-soft cheek with his knuckles. "Feather Light owns this condo. I'm staying here. It was the closest place with a bed."

Her hazel eyes widened. "But I have to go back to work—"

"No. You have to get out of the car, Eden, or else I'm taking you right here on the front seat. Your choice."

Chapter Seven

E DEN COULDN'T MOVE. She stared at the rigid set of Billy's jaw. Need and the underlying darker impression of hunger made his body still, too still, like an agitated jungle cat about to pounce.

Her eyes slid to the condo entrance. Six redwood stairs led to a covered portico. The door was set back far enough into the structure she couldn't discern the color. Besides the scraggly lilac hedge separating the driveway from the sidewalk, they were out in the open. No trees, shade or shadows from nearby buildings. Surely Billy hadn't meant he'd take her right here on the leather seat of his rental car? In broad daylight?

"Well," he demanded. "What's it going to be?"

Holy cow. Guess he *had* meant it.

Before Eden lost her nerve, she grabbed her purse, flung open the door and stumbled out of the car.

Billy was on her before she reached the top step.

He kissed her with an openmouthed mating of tongues—hard,

wet, divine. He pushed her toward the entrance, his body plastered to hers. As he fumbled with the house key, he kissed her. As he struggled to unlock the door, he kissed her. As he opened the door and half-carried, half-dragged her inside, he kept his voracious mouth on hers.

Eden fell headfirst into desire, letting her own long denied needs break free.

"God, I want you," he groaned, slamming the door shut behind them only to flatten her body against the hard surface.

Her purse plunked on the rug. He began a fresh assault on her mouth, little nips and kisses, watching her eyes glaze over while he hurriedly unbuttoned her blouse. The satiny material slid an erotic path down her arms and dropped on the tile.

Then his hands were everywhere.

Sensations bombarded her. His sharp teeth on the swell of her breasts. His shaking hands fumbling with the clasp of her bra. His warm mouth dragging kisses across her moist skin. The ridges of the wooden door digging into her bared back. Her eyes fluttered shut when his lips closed over the peak of her left nipple.

Eager fingers tugged at the side zipper until her skirt met the floor in a soft *whoosh*. Nylons were peeled down her legs, stopped by the barrier of her high-heels. She kicked off her shoes, shed her hosiery. Eden was barefoot and completely naked, except for a damp pair of peach bikini panties.

Ripped out of her sensual daze, she opened her eyes and realized Billy was still fully clothed. She pushed him back a step, her fingers tracing the delineated lines of his chest. One hand unknotted his tie, while the other worked on the buttons of his ivory dress shirt.

Billy toed off his loafers, unfastening his shirt cuffs as she continued to undress him.

"Stand still," she hissed, struggling with his belt buckle. He swayed, trying to remove his socks one-handed. His pants hit the floor, leaving him in boxer briefs and an unbuttoned shirt, looking every inch a male underwear model. She smoothed trembling hands over the golden blond hair dotting his broad chest.

His thumb traced the outline of her lips. "I can't get enough of this mouth."

"Billy—"

"Ssh." His blue eyes were wild, his cheekbones suffused with color. A resigned sigh drifted over her temple as he molded his hard body to her soft curves. "I don't think I can get enough of you, either."

Eden moaned.

Billy swallowed the sound in a greedy kiss. Fingers inched up the inside of her thigh, pushing aside the lace barrier of her panties and plunged into her slick channel, and back out, spreading moisture to the heart of her begging for his attention.

She arched, pushing her pelvis closer, blindly jerking his boxers down his hips to reach for the erection teasing her belly.

He trailed his lips over her jaw. "You are so wet. Do you have any idea what that does to me?"

"Show me."

"Let's go. Condoms are in the bedroom."

"No. Now. Right here, right now." She wrenched away from him and groped on the floor for her purse, coming up with a square package from the inside pocket. She ripped it open with her teeth and shimmied out of her panties.

When Eden looked up, his underwear was history and he stood

before her magnificently naked, strangely vulnerable. She couldn't offer him reassurance that taking this next step wouldn't result in broken promises or broken hearts, nothing but mindless sex. They both knew better.

He helped her roll the condom down the straining length of his cock. Panting against the hollow of her throat, he lifted her higher, pressing her to the door. "Wrap your legs around me."

Eden's arms circled his neck. She dug her heels into the back of his muscular thighs and dropped her hips to feel the tip of his cock demanding entrance to her body.

Billy paused and gazed into her eyes. He lowered his mouth and kissed her at the same time he pushed inside her to the hilt.

His gentle passion nearly undid her.

"Eden." He uttered her name as a reverent sigh. His large hands gripped her butt, tilting her pelvis for the deepest penetration.

What a rush, finally feeling Billy Buchanan inside her body, skin-to-skin, soul-to-soul, man-to-woman. Sweat beaded on her skin. Her mind shut down to everything but pure pleasure.

Billy's controlled thrusts changed to short, hard strokes, which made it impossible to sustain the frantic kiss.

Eden ground into him, her fingers buried in his soft hair, her teeth scraping the rigid cords in his neck. She loved the taste of him on her tongue. The brush of his solid chest against hers. His crisp pubic hair abrading her clit and his firm muscles beneath her hands. The sexy sounds their bodies made at each thrust and retreat.

His forehead dripped sweat on her shoulder and his hips flexed beneath her clenched thighs. Billy shuddered and slowed down, pulling out until just the tip of his cock met the greedy mouth of her sex, then glided back in inch by inch.

"No. Harder." Her heels spurred his butt to remind him to keep up the frenzied pace, cursing his restraint.

Warm lips followed her collarbone. "God. This feels so fucking perfect I can't hold off much longer."

She tilted Billy's face up to meet her eyes. "Don't hold off. I'm right there with you."

Billy's hips began pounding again. Hard. Relentless.

"Yes." Eden's midsection tightened. Her ass slapped into the door with a satisfying sting, and Billy's upper body pressing into hers was the only thing holding her up.

A moment later, she began to come apart. A shiver started in her scalp, zinging through her system like a wayward electrical current.

Billy licked and bit at her neck, his satisfied male chuckle echoed across her skin as tremors rocked her body.

His humor disappeared on a groan.

Feeling drunk from the intensity, her head thunked back. Stars exploded behind her lids.

"Hang on." His hands left her tangled hair and smacked flat beside her head against the door. Four powerful thrusts coaxed another climax from her and she cried out, her vaginal contractions prolonging his release as Billy slammed into her high and hard, growling her name.

Even in the near silence, their harsh breaths, their blood synched as one.

Sweat plastered them to each other and Eden to the door. Several bliss filled seconds passed before she finally whispered, "It was worth the wait."

Chapter Eight

SWEAT DRIPPED INTO Billy's eyes. His toes were cramped and his arms felt like bands of Jell-O.

Beautiful. He'd taken her against the front door. He'd waited ten years and banging Eden fast and furious in the foyer was the best he could offer her?

It was a wonder he ever got laid.

A contented sigh drifted against his neck, followed by a string of openmouthed sucking kisses. Evidently Eden hadn't minded.

Billy leaned back, taking their weight in his legs as he attempted to pull out.

But her thighs gripped him tight. "Stay." She nuzzled his cheek, burying soft lips in the cup of his shoulder. "Just for another minute until my brain can function."

A sense of rightness washed over him. He'd never felt so completely…complete. "You okay? You're not mad that I—"

"—fucked me stupid?" Her lips curved into a smile against his neck. "Are you kidding? I imagined it'd be good between us, but not like that.”

“It was pretty spectacular.”

She shivered delicately and seemed to burrow even deeper into his skin. “You think it was a one shot deal? Years of wondering ‘what-if’ made it impossible *not* to combust when we finally came together?”

He nudged her back against the door, not surprised she’d kept her beautiful eyes closed, hiding her feelings from him. “There’s only one way to find out.”

“How?”

“We have to do it again.” He peppered kisses down her jaw. “And again, and again, and again, until we’re sure it wasn’t a fluke.”

Her laugh soothed his soul.

Billy smoothed an auburn tendril from her flushed cheek. “Eden.”

“Mmm?”

“Baby, look at me.”

She glanced at him from beneath lowered lashes.

“I have to tell you something.”

“No.” She tried to squirm away, an impossible maneuver since they were still physically connected. “Whatever happened in the past doesn’t matter. And if this has to do with the community center, I don’t want to hear it right now, okay?”

He stared at her, the words stuck in his throat. How could he tell her it wasn’t their past that caused his sleepless nights, but thoughts of their future?

“I need to get dressed and go back to work.”

Billy cautioned himself to keep it light as she was already on the verge of retreat. “You sure you can’t stay and play hooky?”

She gave him a sexy grin. "The word you're looking for is *nook-ie*. And no. I have to go."

"Smart-ass." He nipped her chin and she yelped.

"The kids are probably running around driving Shelby crazy with their questions about where I am."

"Are you there every day after school?"

"Without fail." Eden's fingers trailed a path across his shoulders and her mouth tasted the skin she'd touched.

Another whip of desire cracked through him. "Then you deserve a break. Stay. Please."

"Tempting…but no." She whacked his butt and he withdrew from the warm place that strangely felt like home.

When her feet touched the tile, she shivered and bent to grab her clothes, muttering, "Looks like a damn yard sale in here."

Billy plucked up his clothing on the way to dispose of the condom. In the bathroom, he peered at his reflection, turning his profile left and right. Yep. Same guy on the outside, but the emotions jumping inside told a different tale. The last few days he'd been revitalized.

Scrubbing his hands over his face, he slumped back against the wall. *Face the facts, man.* His return to Spearfish hadn't been about helping out an old friend or an excuse to checkup on his sister. He'd come back for her. Now that he realized the magnitude of the mistake he'd made years ago, how could he walk away? Now that he was certain she'd always been *the* one for him?

Worse yet, if he loved her, how could he close the center?

A soft rapping on the door ripped him from his reverie. "Billy? Look, I hate to screw and run, but I've got to get back."

He grinned at her phrasing, hoping it indicated there'd be no awkward silences between them on the drive back to the center.

EDEN PRIMLY CROSSED her bare legs. She hadn't bothered putting her nylons back on. As she surveyed the landscape out the window of the rental car, she sensed Billy's confusion. He'd tried to delve into what'd happened and she'd blatantly ignored him. And she'd practically jumped from his car when he pulled up at the community center.

Shelby didn't pester her about the overly long lunch but Eden's relief was short-lived. She'd nearly ducked into the safety of her office when a soft voice startled her.

"Aha! I knew I'd catch you goofing off someday."

Eden faced her friend, Tate LeBeau. "As you can see, I'm back at the grindstone."

Tate's blue eyes turned shrewd. "What's up with those rosy cheeks and sparkling eyes?" Her gaze traveled up Eden's exposed shins and narrowed on a spot below her ear.

Dammit. Had Billy given her a hickey? Ten years ago he'd delighted in marking her as his, everywhere, but he'd outgrown that impulse, hadn't he? Eden resisted the urge to rub her neck.

Unfortunately, Billy chose that moment to saunter around the corner. His contented smirk disappeared and he stopped dead in his tracks. Eden suspected their guilt was obvious.

"Oh my God. Billy Buchanan? Is that really you?"

"In the flesh."

Tate rushed forward, blond hair flying as she enveloped him in a hug. "It's good to see you, even though I haven't forgiven you for leaving Nathan in the lurch all those years ago." She whapped him lightly on the arm. "Poor man was forced to finish the fire station project all by himself."

Billy had the grace to blush. "I wish I'd had another choice." His troubled gaze connected with Eden's before he gave Tate a boyish grin. "You look exactly the same."

She patted her pregnant belly. "Not exactly."

"Dare I ask how many kids make up the LeBeau household these days?"

"This one is number five." With pride she rattled off, "Sophie is seven, Ben is five, the twins, Michael and Sasha are three."

He whistled. "Been a busy decade. How is Nathan?"

Tate beamed the pure sunshine of a woman wildly in love. "Wonderful. Business is great. He has four fulltime employees, which means he has time to coach the kids' various sports teams and knock me up on a regular basis."

When Eden attempted to sneak into her office to let them catch up, Tate firmly grabbed her elbow. "Excuse us. Eden and I have some…ah, issues to discuss." She propelled Eden into the office, slammed the door and clicked the metal blinds shut.

No escape. Pregnancy hormones seemed to have given Tate super-human strength and eagle-eyed detection skills. "Spill it, girl. How long have you been sleeping with Billy?"

Eden didn't bother to lie; Tate knew her too well. "Since about an hour ago." She skirted the desk but was too wired to sit. "Don't start." During Eden's teenage years, Tate had become her mentor at the community center. Eleven years later, Tate was still a mentor, but also a close friend, so Tate was aware of Eden's devastation when Billy had abruptly left her life.

"You expecting a lecture? From me? You know better. No bull. What is going on?"

"If I tell you I don't know, will you believe me?"

"Yes." Tate's eyes softened. "Talk to me."

The words tumbled out in a rush. "This is all so surreal. Get this: Billy's working for Feather Light, deciding the future of the community center, which means my future is in his hands." She inhaled a deep yoga breath to keep the hysteria at bay. "But from the minute Billy walked in the door, it hasn't been about business, or my future, but our past."

"I imagine that drives you crazy."

"Not only haven't I seen any of his notes regarding the center, I have to deal with my stupid hormones wanting to get naked with him. All. The. Damn. Time. When he smiles at me, every professional thought sails right out of my head." A shiver moved through her. "Maybe I'm more like my mother than I want to admit."

Memories of men parading out of her mother's room in the early morning hours flashed in Eden's mind. Whenever her mother stared into space, mooning over some new guy she'd met at work, inevitably her mom lost her job.

"Eden LaCroix, you are nothing like your mother," Tate muttered. "Although sometimes I wish you were."

Her astonished gaze snapped back to Tate. "What?"

"You're so caught up in making sure your reputation in this community is beyond reproach, you've forgotten there's more to life than work. No one will begrudge you a relationship."

"With the man who's come here to shut down the community center?" Eden said incredulously. "How could I ever explain my way out of that?"

"Billy already told you he's closing you down?"

"No. Whenever he gets within three feet of me, we both forget the real reason he's here." But he'd mentioned concrete concerns in the car. Had he been serious? Or angling for an excuse to relive their delicious lunch? Sad thing was, it wouldn't take much to convince her she should spend all of her meals with him, stripped bare and screaming for another course.

"Regardless of the business end of things, he still cares for you," Tate said.

"You can't know that. You've seen him for what? Two minutes?"

"So?"

"So, neither of us is the same person we were ten years ago." Eden glanced at her framed college diploma, then at the high school one hanging beside it. "We can't go back."

"But you don't want to go forward either. For years you've used your experience with Billy as an excuse not to get involved with any man." Tate held up her hand, stopping Eden's protest. "And no, banging Jon White Feather like a drum whenever the mood strikes you does *not* count, because both you and Jon use your pasts as an excuse not to move on—either together or separately."

Stupid insightful pregnancy hormones.

"Now that Billy has returned, apparently willing to make amends to you or to change your opinion of him, you're unwilling to do either."

Eden barely held on to her temper. "What do you expect me to do? Blindly give him my heart and my trust again?"

"Sweetie. Why won't you admit he's *always* had your heart?"

Dammit. She refused to respond.

"Lord, you are stubborn as a mule. Seems no matter what Billy does or doesn't do, he can't win."

"You're defending him?"

"No, I'm pointing out the facts. If Billy doesn't close the community center, you won't believe he didn't do it to get in your good graces. If Billy does recommend closing it, you have a legitimate reason not to pursue a relationship with him."

"What relationship? He lives in Chicago. I live in Spearfish. This 'relationship' is nothing but another loose end he's tying up while he's here."

Tate studied her face until Eden squirmed under the intensity. "Think about what you really want and don't be such a chickenshit about going after it." Then Tate was gone.

Eden slumped in her office chair. She was no closer to knowing what her future held than she was three days ago.

She did know one thing for certain—ten years of life experience only added to Billy's appeal. Yet, she suspected when it was all said and done he'd walk away. Unscathed. Just like he had before.

Despite Tate's observation Billy carried a torch for her, she didn't believe he wanted more than a mutual slaking of lust. Her feelings for him were her problem. But she'd be damned if she'd spend time brooding about it. Life went on.

Eden flipped on her computer and lost herself in work while she still had a job.

A LUSH MALE voice sang, "Knock, knock, knockin' on heaven's door…"

Eden looked up and smiled at the longhaired, leather-clad Indian casually leaning against the doorjamb.

Simply put, Jon White Feather was a beautiful man. His angular face, courtesy of his Swedish mother, was as striking as his pale blue eyes. His broad forehead sloped into high, wide cheekbones. A regal nose gave way to lush lips and a pointed chin. Copper-colored skin bespoke his Lakota heritage. Tall, muscularly lean, his meaty biceps and the insides of his forearms were decorated with tribal tattoos. His black hair flowed past his shoulders, giving him the look of a bad boy rocker mixed with an Indian warrior. He was built, he was hot and his intense gaze still made her belly quiver after years of friendship. "*Hoka-hey, kola.*"

"Jon. I was wondering when you'd get into town."

He quirked a dark eyebrow at her. "You haven't seen me in six months and that's my welcome? How about some sugar from my best girl, eh?" He spread his arms wide.

She skirted the desk and launched herself at him. Jon spun her in a circle amidst her laughter.

"Didja miss me, my wicked little garden sprite?"

"No."

He whispered, "Liar."

"Fine. I missed you. Put me down."

"Only if you promise to go out with me tomorrow night."

"Where?" The last time she'd forgotten to ask specifics she'd ended up in a strip club in Wyoming with Jon and six of his bruiser roadies, watching them jump into a bar fight with a group of hot cowboys. After the blood and the insults dried up, the dozen or so guys had shot whiskey in the tour bus until dawn.

"How about someplace off the beaten track?"

When he rolled into town, Jon preferred to lay low somewhere he wouldn't be recognized. "Like the Silver Star?" The honky-tonk was one of the few places in town that didn't cater to college students.

"I'll probably be the only Indian in the place amidst cowboy hats and shitkickers, and you know what happened last time, but it's a deal."

She returned to her chair while Jon flopped across from her desk. "So what're you doing at the community center? Working out that buff bod of yours?"

Jon gifted her with a smoldering look. "I'm here just for you, dollface."

"Wrong. Try again."

"Man. I can't pull nothin' over on you." He grinned pure mischief. "I told Jim I'd pick up Micah from basketball practice since Cindy is dealing with sick kids. But I really did volunteer so I could pop in and see what you were up to."

Eden gestured at the piles. "The usual."

"You work too hard, which is why I'm taking you out for a night of fun. How long's it been since you cut loose?"

"Months. I've had a lot on my mind."

"I heard. Jim says the center might be in trouble. What's up with that?"

"The same old bullshit. It's been coming for a year so I'm not surprised."

He frowned. "Is your job in jeopardy?"

"Yeah." She looked away to avoid his pity.

Papers rustled as Jon leaned across her desk and clasped her hand in his. "Hey. If the city is stupid enough to let you go, their loss, eh?"

Underneath Jon's sexy persona of rocker Johnny Feather lurked a really sweet, thoughtful guy. "I guess."

"You could always go on the road with me."

"What would my job be?"

"My personal love slave."

Eden snorted. "You've already got that position filled. They're called groupies."

Jon brought her hand to his mouth and kissed her knuckles. "None of them hold a candle to you."

"Flatterer. But I will take it under consideration if this place goes belly up." She threaded her fingers through his. "How long are you here?"

He sighed. "Only two days. This break isn't near long enough."

"And you say I work too hard?"

"Yeah, well, I'd like to hang out to catch up with Jim and his tribe, but unfortunately, most of my time will be spent in Eagle Butte."

"Another last minute gig?"

"No. My bass guitarist is getting married." He dropped his gaze to their joined hands. "I oughta be thrilled for him, right? His woman is awesome. He's never been happier."

"But?"

"That's the thing. But nothin'. Him getting hitched won't adversely affect the band, so it's not a professional issue. I can't figure out why I'm…pissed. Frustrated."

"Jealous?" Eden offered.

"Maybe." Jon's thumb stroked the inside of her wrist. "He's the first one of the band members to pair off. Which is cool. When he's with her, it's like they're the only two people in the world, even if there's a dozen people on the bus. I'm surrounded by people almost twenty-four/seven so why do I always feel so damn lonely?"

Eden was familiar with that feeling, but as this was one of the few times Jon had opened up in recent years, she didn't interrupt.

"Do you ever look around at your life and feel like you're missing out on what's really important, even when you aren't sure what that important something might be?"

"Yeah. We all have days like that."

"Some of us more than others. I just wish…"

"What?" When his startling blue eyes connected with hers, her stomach cartwheeled.

"I forget how beautiful you are."

Her face heated and she yanked her hand back. "Jon. Stop."

"I'm serious, Eden. You're beautiful. Smart. Successful. Funny as hell. Sweet as pie when you ain't bein' a pain in the ass." His grin was there and gone. "You've dealt with the same Indian/white racist shit I have. The sex between us is great. My family adores you. *I* adore you."

"I assume this sweet talk has a point, *kola*?"

"Sometimes I don't just want to be your friend, Eden. I want more." His eyes went from playful to haunted. "You are the perfect woman for me. So why can't I settle down with you and let you fill the lonely spots in my life?"

"A—because you aren't ready to abandon your wicked rocker ways and pledge your life to one woman. B—because you snore. C—because you don't love me."

"I should. You'd be good for me."

"Would you be good for me, Jon?" Eden asked softly.

"No." Jon sighed again. "It wouldn't be fair because I don't know if I can ever…" He briefly shut his eyes. "You deserve so much more than the pittance I can offer you, *winyan*."

Eden's heart clenched at the raw pain in his melodic voice. "Are you ever going to forgive yourself? It wasn't your fault Juliette died."

"Yeah, it was."

They'd had this conversation dozens of times and it always ended the same way: with Jon changing the subject.

"You're one of the few people in my life who doesn't automatically say, 'Yes, Johnny' to whatever crazy thing I suggest. Not only do you know the real me—Jon the half-breed Indian with a checkered past—but you don't want anything from me."

"Except hot sex," she teased, hoping to lighten his mood.

"But even that is different, truer, than with the groupies hanging around, waiting to fuck me in the tour bus strictly for the bragging rights that they nailed Johnny Feather."

"The price of being semi-famous."

"Price," he scoffed. "My agent, the promoters, the tour director, the radio stations, the assorted tribes, the fans; they all see me as a commodity. Dollar signs. A brand. It gets old."

Eden didn't say anything.

Jon grimaced. "Listen to me. I have everything I ever dreamed of as a poor kid on the rez and I'm complaining? You probably think I'm a self-indulgent prick, eh?"

"No, I think you need a friend."

"Thanks. You are a damn good friend, Eden, and I missed you." He kissed her knuckles again before releasing her hand. "But we're still friends with bennies, right? Because I'm about a quart low on sweet lovin'."

What kind of woman even considers a round of no-strings-sex with one guy mere hours after screwing another one?

The answer was a stab in her gut, *the kind of woman who raised you. You're just like your mother.*

"Eden?"

She smiled tightly. "The truth is, I'm sort of seeing someone."

"Anyone I know?"

"No."

"Is it serious?"

Eden shrugged.

"Doesn't matter. I still wanna hang out with you while I'm here." Jon gave her a shrewd look. "Tell you what. Bring him along tomorrow night. I'll check him out to see if he's good enough for my best girl."

And wouldn't that be an awkward situation? *Billy, meet Johnny. Johnny and I play naked Indian poke-her whenever he rolls into town. Johnny, meet Billy. Billy is here to fuck up my life on a professional level, but that doesn't matter because I let him fuck me any other way he pleases.*

"What's goin' on in that pretty head of yours?" Jon murmured.

"Nothing. Just wondering if I should pick you up at Jim and Cindy's tomorrow night?"

"Nah. Bebe and Stephie are both sick so I'm not staying with them. I'm crashing at Jim's old condo."

Eden frowned. Something about that seemed familiar.

"I'll meet you. Silver Star at seven?"

"Deal."

"You dressing up full-on bad boy rock star?" Eden asked slyly.

"Nope. I'm sticking with the poor Indian look. So don't be surprised if you don't recognize me."

"Right, dollface," Eden repeated his oft-used term of endearment. "You could wear sackcloth and ashes and you'd still be the hottest guy in the room and you damn well know it."

"Now who's the flatterer?"

Micah and Thomas burst in, dribbling a basketball, creating chaos and Eden was grateful for the diversion.

Chapter Nine

BILLY'S WORKDAY WAS a lost cause.

His focus centered around reliving Eden's husky moans of delight as he slid in and out of her slick feminine heat, the satisfying weight of her lissome body wrapped around his, the remembrance of her sweet and hot kisses. Occasionally he'd catch a whiff of her scent on his skin and he'd go as hard as his protractor.

Before he'd left Bob's office, he'd grudgingly grabbed the files concerning the community center. The logical thing would be to hole up and decide on a course of action for the city council.

Sometimes logic was highly overrated.

Almost on autopilot, Billy drove to the community center. He justified the burning need to see her because they had business to discuss, preferably in a room without a bed.

He winced. That hadn't seemed to matter a few hours ago when he'd taken her hard and fast against the front door.

No regrets, but there hadn't been any finesse either.

Her Jeep was parked in its usual spot and he wasn't surprised she was working late. Briefcase in hand, he passed by the gym, stopping to observe a raucous basketball game. The men appeared to be his age, but that didn't stop the cheap shots or the adolescent taunts. After a nasty elbow jab, in the next play, the jabber found himself facedown on the court courtesy of the jabbee.

Billy squinted at the kid leaning against the back wall. Was that Thomas? He waved.

But Thomas didn't wave back. A stricken look crossed the kid's face and he disappeared beneath the wooden bleachers.

Dammit. According to Eden, Thomas wasn't supposed to be here this time of night. Had he snuck in again? It made Billy absolutely sick to think the kid had to figure out a way to avoid getting a beating on a regular basis. He suspected Eden's bond with Thomas was partially because she'd been in that same "duck and run" family situation. Billy's childhood hadn't been ideal, but physical violence hadn't been an issue. So did he keep Thomas's secret so the kid would be safe tonight? Or did Billy tell Eden he'd spied her young friend hiding out again?

The empty corridors were quiet, save for the far-off mechanical whine of a vacuum cleaner and the shuffle of his hard soled dress shoes on the marble floor. Light shone through the half-closed blinds in Eden's office.

He knocked and heard a brusque, "Come in."

Billy hesitated on the threshold. "Am I interrupting?"

"Would it matter?"

"No."

"Why are you here?"

"I need to talk to you."

A deliberate pause. "Is this a matter concerning the center?"

Concerning the center. No surprise she wouldn't discuss their mind-scrambling sex that'd ruined him for any other woman. "Actually, yes, I do have some questions." He slid into the chair opposite her desk and opened his briefcase, shuffling through the papers until he found the one he needed. "My research shows nothing's been done with the electrical system since the city took over this building twenty-five years ago?"

"We've hired an electrician to put in additional outlets or fix some minor glitch, but as far as major rework? Not in the five years I've been in charge. Why?"

"Seems the city only did minimal changes back then," he said, scanning his notes.

"Didn't it pass inspection?"

"Yes, but neither the city nor the contractor kept a detailed list of what'd been updated. My understanding is that this building was a temporary solution, so they only made the most rudimentary updates."

"Which means…?" Eden looked at him expectantly.

"A whole different set of unforeseen problems with wiring codes."

"I don't understand. How can you assume the wiring is faulty if you can't see it?"

Billy snapped the briefcase shut, using it as a lap desk. "That's the crux of the problem. The only way we can determine whether the wiring is coated with asbestos is to rip out all the walls. And if we rip out all the walls…"

"The city might as well rip out everything and start from scratch." Her glance darted to the fire alarm across the room. "Is there a danger of an electrical fire?"

"Certainly it's a possibility."

Eden mulled it over. "What the hell else can go wrong?"

The bitterness in her tone didn't surprise him. If his livelihood were at stake he imagined he'd be testy, too. "The family who owns the land has no interest in buying the building. It's a tricky situation when the landowner and the building owner aren't the same party, but I've seen this type of situation before—where one party puts land in a trust and another party builds on it in the guise of civic improvement."

"Have you spoken with the landowners?"

"No. It seemed irrelevant. Why?"

Eden's shrug was nonchalant, yet her fingers folded a neon post-it-note as if she was practicing origami. "Rumor has it if the city's findings are against improving the center, and they level the building, the landowners will use the lot and the empty one directly behind us to construct a fitness center that'd be in direct competition with the city's new digs."

Billy smiled, even if it felt a bit grim. "No love lost, huh?"

"No. I'm surprised the land trust agreement hasn't been challenged in court. Not only have the council members been bickering among themselves about this situation for years, the family owning the land has been stuck dealing with the bureaucracy."

"Have the landowners asked you to get involved if they do build the new facility?"

"Probably they won't, since I am a city employee. They'll assume I have a job." She sighed. "I hate politics. My main concern, my only concern, has been how this will affect the kids."

Devoted to others needs before her own—that was Eden to the core. He paused to gather his thoughts in the pretext of double-checking his notes. When he glanced up, she was rubbing her temple. "You okay?"

"Makes my head hurt thinking about this stuff."

"I'm not trying to give you a headache, Eden. I'm just trying to do my job."

A second passed. Then two. If this were a normal relationship, Billy supposed he'd cross the room, gather her in his arms and offer reassurances. So why was his dumb ass still glued to this cheap chair? Why were his hands still gripping his hard leather briefcase instead of her soft curves? He scooted forward, determined to prove this "thing" happening between them could be permanent and he was finally man enough to stand up for what he wanted: her.

But it wasn't her voice that stopped him cold; it was her utter look of defeat. "So what do we do now?"

"Have you eaten?"

"I'm not hungry. I had a late lunch."

Their gazes locked. "I know. I was there, remember?"

Eden opened her mouth then snapped it shut.

"Can we talk about our lunch date today?"

"No." She wheeled back and stood, snatching her keys from her desk. "Did I answer all of your questions? Because I—"

Billy was next to her before she could retreat. "Don't do this, Eden. Don't pretend nothing changed between us and we're just opposing sides in a business disagreement."

"What do you want me to do? Ignore it?"

"Yes." Billy tilted her chin up. "Put it aside. Just for tonight. Be with me. Let me come home with you."

Her eyes darkened with reproach as he leaned close enough to kiss her. "Not here—"

"Then invite me over. Please." He swept a tangled strand of hair from the corner of her mouth. "I want to be with you."

Eden twirled her car keys on her index finger. "Who the hell am I kidding? I want to be with you too. Let me lock up."

"While you're locking up, I think we should look for Thomas. I thought I saw him in the gym."

"That little sneak. He knows he's not supposed to be here this late. I'll check his usual hiding spots and meet you at my house."

"Do you need help?"

"No. Actually it'd be better if you left. He might stay hidden if he sees you."

"Be careful."

Chapter Ten

EDEN DIDN'T FIND Thomas, but she'd managed to get filthy while looking. She jumped in the shower and didn't bother getting dressed afterward. No sense pretending they wouldn't be naked together within minutes anyway.

Carnal images of red-hot pleasure ran through her head, heating her blood so the cool water practically sizzled on her naked skin. She imagined the prickle of Billy's beard rubbing between her thighs. His rough fingertips trailing over every dip and swell of her body. His clever mouth doing all sorts of clever things.

Stop. If her thoughts traveled that route, she'd melt into a puddle right there on the bath mat. She tightened the belt on her robe and ventured downstairs. Billy was gazing out the living room window.

"Nice neighborhood."

"Thanks."

"This is a great house. How long have you lived here?"

Eden pressed her face into the middle of his back, wrapping her arms low on his hips. She inhaled. Mmm. The scent drifting from him ought to be classified as dangerous because it certainly made her reckless. "Did you really come over so we could talk about real estate?"

"No."

"The romp this afternoon wasn't enough?"

"If I say *no* will you think I'm a sex fiend?"

She laughed. "No. I'll chalk it up to ten years of wondering how it'd be between us becoming reality. We'd be stupid not to explore every down and dirty sexy fantasy we denied ourselves now that we have the chance."

His back snapped straight. "That's what it boils down to? This is just about sex?"

"For tonight it is." She grabbed his shoulders from behind, pulling him down so her teeth could nip his earlobe. "I want you."

Billy faced her. "Eden—"

"Let me have you." She smoothed her hands up the crisp navy cotton of his shirt. "It's a damn shame I haven't taken my time undressing you."

"We have all the time in the world. Let's take it upstairs."

"No. Here." She closed the blinds. By the time Eden's fingers reached the last pearly button near his groin, she saw Billy was having difficulty breathing. She slowly parted the halves of the shirt, gliding her soft hands over the breadth of his chest. So solid. So rough and silky at the same time.

Her lips followed the path her fingers started. She slipped the shirt off his shoulders, down his muscular biceps and forearms until it fluttered to the floor. "You don't spend all your time behind a desk." She steeped her senses in his scent, laundry soap, a hint of aftershave and the musk of his skin. Her tongue flicked the flat coppery disk of his nipple.

Billy groaned.

So she did it again. And again. Sucking both sides. Worrying the nubs with her teeth.

His groan was louder. Primal.

She skimmed her fingertips from his Adam's apple to his navel, loving how his belly muscles undulated beneath her touch.

"Eden. Baby."

"Ssh. No talking." Eden kissed his stomach. She dipped her tongue into his belly button and drew big, wet circles progressively lower. She licked the faint line of blond hair pointing to her target.

"This looks promising." She unbuttoned his pants to reveal the ultimate precision engineering tool.

Oh yeah. Eden knew just how to fine-tune this bad boy. She didn't tease. She sucked his cock into the wet heat of her mouth until the plump tip poked the back of her throat.

"Jesus." He latched onto her head and threaded his hands through her hair.

"Mmm," was all she managed, lost in the slick sensation of velvety male hardness sliding across her lips, looking up, seeing the raw need in his eyes. She let the end of her tongue zigzag lazily from his scrotum to his glans, licking at the tip of his cock.

"That's so good. Woman, you're killing me."

Then she slipped her hand between his thighs to massage his balls, pressing her thumb into the strip of skin right behind the taut sac. She loved everything about this intimacy. The musky male way he smelled. His clean, salty taste. The feel of the hardest part of him stretching her lips and brushing the roof of her mouth. His tiny shudders when she lapped the sweet spot below his cockhead and at the sweet fluid coating the slit.

"You want to come fast or slow?"

"Ah. Fast. Christ. Please."

Eden circled her hand around the base of his shaft and jacked him while her mouth counter-stroked, lips and fingers meeting in the middle. Her head bobbing, her mouth watering, her teeth-scraping, all rhythmic sucking, heat and wetness. Worshiping that marvelous male flesh.

Billy's hips pumped. His thumbs spread across her hollowed cheeks as she took him deeper yet. The wet, sucking sounds of her mouth on his sex and his answering moans of ecstasy made her thighs sticky and her blood race.

"Eden. Stop or I'm gonna shoot."

"Shoot in my mouth, Billy."

A low growl rumbled from his chest. "Then you'll swallow every goddamn drop." His hands returned to her head and he gripped hanks of hair in his fists, adding an erotic pinch of pain as he fucked her mouth.

His body tensed. "Here it comes." His cock lifted slightly, the length tightened and twitched as pulse after pulse of hot come flowed over her tongue and dripped down the back of her throat.

She kept swallowing, stroking, wringing every ounce of pleasure from him until he begged, "Stop. Jesus. I can't take any more, baby," and his spent cock slipped from her mouth.

Billy hadn't opened his eyes. His hands were clenched into fists by his naked flanks. A beautiful red flush colored his cheeks and his breathing was decidedly ragged.

Good.

Quietly, Eden stood and padded to the kitchen. Her hand shook so badly that she spilled water down her neck. The cold glass felt heavenly against her hot lips. Liquid cooled her mouth but washed away the taste of him.

She heard his footfalls stop on the linoleum behind her.

Billy pulled her against his chest. "That was fucking amazing," he muttered gruffly.

"For me too. Are you hungry?"

"Only hungry for you, Eden." His lips brushed her ear. "I want you."

"But—"

"Stop talking. Let me have you."

Amidst drugging kisses, his thumbs feathered touches on her stomach near her belly button and the muscles rippled in response.

"Hang on." Then he lifted her onto the counter. "Take off the robe. Now."

"Right here? In the kitchen?"

"You just had me in the living room." The heat in his eyes contrasted with the gentle hands he placed on her collarbones. "So yes. Right here, right now." His mouth sought hers and he oh-so-slowly lowered the robe, allowing the silky material to slither over her bared back.

As he cranked up the kiss, his hands drifted across the slopes of her breasts, slipping over her torso and briefly landing on her midriff. Billy grabbed her butt, tugging her half-on, half-off the counter.

Eden jerked back. "I'm falling."

"I won't let you." Sweaty palms glided over the breadth of her legs to her knees. He watched her eyes as he splayed her thighs apart. "Put your hands behind you and dig your heels into the cabinet door."

"But—"

"Do it," he growled, shutting her up with another carnal kiss that curled her toes, her hair and her internal organs.

When he ripped his mouth free, the desire in his eyes almost toppled her off the counter.

Billy warned, "Brace yourself," and dropped to his knees on the rug in front of her.

Every bit of blood drained from Eden's upper body, plummeting to the lower regions currently *not* in need of additional blood flow.

He clamped his fingers securely around her quaking knees and rubbed his mouth there. "Jesus, you smell good." His labored breathing echoed hers as he wended his way toward his target via the inside of her thigh. The slow, steady rasp of his razor-stubbled jaw made her squirm. After one quick swipe at the throbbing center of her heat, he nibbled a path to the other knee.

A frustrated sigh escaped her.

Billy repeated the teasing tactic on her legs, getting closer with each wet pass of his tongue, until Eden groaned at the erotic combination of his soft hair and hot mouth brushing her hypersensitive skin.

Finally Billy's tongue darted out for a thorough taste of her pussy, probing, licking and then retreating before he blew one soft breath over her molten core.

"You are so wet. So hot. So unbelievably delicious." He continued torturing her with smallest flicks of the tip of his tongue. "Mmm. Same pretty pink color here as your mouth. It was hot as hell seeing my cock disappearing between your sweet lips." He detoured and licked the crease of her thigh.

Eden's leg spasmed involuntarily and he chuckled, the low rumble shot a spike of heat from her groin to her nipples. But Billy avoided the area where Eden craved his elusive tongue.

Her breath sawed in and out of her lungs. Sweat dampened her neck, her back, between her legs. She wanted to plunge her hands in his silky hair and force his wandering head closer.

"Such soft skin right here," he whispered, nipping at the curve of her inner thigh, while his thumbs drew feathery circles behind her knees. He tortured her with openmouthed kisses down the front of her shin to her ankle.

Not up.

Damn him.

Billy licked the shallow dent near her heel; his fingertips stroked the back of her calf. Lightly. Like raindrops. He nibbled the top of her twitching foot, then set his hot mouth right above her anklebone and sucked.

"Oh. My. God." Eden's eyes rolled back in her head. Whoa. Since when was her ankle an erogenous zone with a hyperlink to her burning pussy?

"Like that, do you?"

He did it again and her sex contracted.

A small scream burst from Eden's throat. "Billy, I thought you said no more talking. And there you are, *jabbering* for God's sake—"

"Fine. I'm done." His tongue blazed up her channel, making her wetter and wetter. Stopping to suckle her swollen pussy lips. Swirling that naughty tongue in circles. Fast. Slow. Teasing. Blatant.

Billy pressed his thumbs above her pubic bone, peeled back the hood hiding that little bud, and fastened his mouth to her clit. He used his lips, his teeth—God—his *tongue*—persistently until she thought she'd burst.

And she did, climaxing in a flash, gasping his name as he sucked and sucked. The pounding, pulsing waves flared from her sex, sending shudders of pleasure throughout her whole body.

Sated, dazed, spent, Eden forgot about bracing herself and let her head fall back in utter abandon. The resounding whack against the cupboard and sharp pain barely registered.

When the tremors stopped, she gazed down at him.

His blue eyes were ablaze, his mouth glistening with her juices. "Remember the other night? When I told you what I wanted from you?"

His explicit words rang in her ears, promises of exactly what he planned to do to her. "Uh. Yeah."

"I'm gonna take you that way tonight. Now."

Pulling her from the counter, Billy rocked his erection into her pelvis and captured her mouth with a wet, soul-sucking kiss. He detached his lips from hers. "Go upstairs. Get your vibrator. And a towel. I have to get something and then I'll be right up."

Chapter Eleven

AFTER TAKING THE condoms from his pocket, Billy left his clothes where he'd shed them and headed upstairs.

A small light on the nightstand suffused the room with soft amber light. Eden had rolled down the bedspread and was sprawled in the center of the mattress.

He stopped and stared. "You steal my breath."

But her eyes were glued on the bottle of oil in his hand.

Billy set the stuff next to the vibrator and perched on the edge of the bed. "Hey." He smoothed his hand from the curve of her shoulder to her wrist. "You okay?"

"Ah. Yeah. What's the oil for?"

Keeping his gaze on hers, he traced her index finger in a sensual line from the nail to the knuckle and across the webbing, eliciting her deep shiver. "You know what it's for." He leaned forward and kissed her, a slow tango of sliding lips and dueling tongues.

The kiss changed from sweet, to hot, to molten. Gentle caresses turned into uncontrolled touches. Billy ended up on top of Eden, with his hand buried between her soft, damp thighs. God. She was wet again. He wanted her so badly it was painful.

"I can't wait. On your hands and knees."

Eden didn't look at him as she rolled over.

Billy slipped on a condom, grabbed the vibrator and placed it next to her right hand on the bed. He caged her body below his and put his lips on her ear. "Do you know how incredible you look? With your ass in the air waiting for me? It's sexy as hell. I'll go slowly. Nothing to be scared of." When he nuzzled her nape, she trembled. "Nothing to be ashamed of either, Eden."

"I know. I want this. I want this with you." She turned her head and nipped his jaw. "Do it. Take the last of my virginity, Billy."

Somehow he kept from ramming his cock into her right then. He set his hand in the middle of her back and pushed her upper body flat on the bed. "Be easier for you to use the vibrator in this position. Now spread your knees wider. Tilt your hips up. Oh, yeah. Perfect."

The little pucker and her pussy were completely visible, a wet, pink oasis amidst the tawny skin of her rounded ass and slender thighs. His cock went hard as a ruler.

He reached for the bottle of vegetable oil and tipped it, dribbling the liquid down her ass crack.

"Oh. That's warm."

"I heated it." He cupped oil in his hand, using some on his cock and the rest to coat his fingers. He probed the tiny hole with one finger, added more oil, inserted another finger and poured the remainder a little at a time as his fingers fucked in and out of her untried ass.

Eden shuddered.

"You okay?"

"Yes. Just do it."

For a second he couldn't focus beyond his animalistic lust, his need, the male possession thumping in his chest. But somehow he held off impaling her to the hilt in one lightning fast stroke. "Just a little more." He scissored his fingers inside her narrow opening to stretch her, bowled over by the tight, slick heat. When Eden pumped her hips back with a whimper, he knew she was ready.

Billy slowly circled the plump head of his cock around the slippery entrance, knowing the stimulation of pressure on the nerve-endings would drive her crazy. Then he popped just the cockhead in and stopped.

"Oh God."

"No, baby, don't clench. Does it hurt?"

"Yeah, but keep going."

I'll show you how I can keep going. Harder. Faster. Make you burn. Prove to you who this ass and everything attached to it belongs to; always has, always will.

Reason shoved the male glutton aside. *No. Hold off, hold off, hold off, don't be a brute, don't be selfish. Be the tender man she deserves.*

"Billy?"

"I can't reach your clit. Do you want to slide the vibrator in your pussy before I'm in fully?"

"No. God. Please. Just finish what you started."

"Then say it. Say the words, Eden."

"Fill my ass."

"I love it when you talk dirty." He eased all the way into that tight, hot channel and groaned. Damn. He wasn't going to last long even if he wasn't moving much. Even if he wanted to pull her ass cheeks apart and ream her, watching that small hole stretching to accommodate his dick. Feel that close-fitting heat sucking him in, the tight muscles milking him dry, making him mindless with lust.

"Why did you stop?"

"Because it feels so damn good I want to savor it. You're like silk inside, Eden. Warm, tight, hot silk around my cock."

The buzz of the vibrator brought him out of his pleasure stupor. When she rested the phallus against the length of her pussy and Billy felt the vibration in his balls, his hips snapped back and he plunged to the hilt again.

The noise from her sweet mouth was indistinguishable as pleasure or pain so he kept the next few strokes measured. Rivulets of sweat snaked down his temple. His molars damn near cracked from clenching his jaw. His fingers gripped Eden's curvy hips in an effort not to fuck her virgin ass like a wild man.

He tried to concentrate on the sweet perfume of her arousal not the supreme tightness of her anal passage. The sight and sound of her arm moving between her legs as she pleasured herself. How perfectly her ass muscles clenched and unclenched around his cock. The brightness of her auburn hair flowing across the pristine white sheet. How erotic his cock looked disappearing between those softly rounded bronze cheeks.

But it didn't help. His awareness was solely in his dick and the *tight hot tight hot tight hot faster faster faster* mantra urging him to plow into her ass. He gave in. One hard, deep thrust from cockhead to root.

"Just like that. Do it like that again. Fuck my ass harder, I'm so close—"

Eden didn't finish the sentence before Billy jackhammered into her tight portal over and over.

When Eden began to come, gasping, thrusting her hips back, her anal muscles contracting, the vibrator buzzing near his balls, Billy lost it. He fucked her without pause, lost in that *yes yes yes* blur of unconsciousness, where nothing mattered but expelling every ounce of hot seed into those clenching walls.

What a fucking rush. Like being in a Formula One car, bungee jumping into a gorge and on the steepest drop of a roller coaster—all at the same time.

After he reclaimed his brain cells from pleasure overload, Billy kissed his way up Eden's spine. "That was amazing."

"I…damn. I don't even know what to say."

"You okay?" he murmured.

"Yeah. Tired. You wore me out today, Billy."

"Mmm." He tasted the sweat on her neck and softly blew in her ear to distract her while he pulled his semi-soft cock out of her ass.

Eden hissed.

He scattered more soft kisses across her shoulder. "Be right back."

A few minutes later, he brought a warm washcloth. He cleaned her up amidst flirty kisses, thorough caresses and whispering sweet words against her sweet-smelling skin. Billy couldn't get enough of touching her, running his hands and mouth over every inch of her sleek curves. He hauled her upper body across his, continuing to drag his fingertips up and down her spine.

Eden propped her chin on his chest and gave him a pensive look. "I have to ask you something kinda weird."

He twirled a section of her hair around his finger. "What?"

"Would you like to go to the Silver Star tomorrow night?"

"Is it a restaurant?"

"No. It's a bar. There's music and dancing."

"I thought you preferred to keep our relationship off the radar."

"That's why it'd be perfect. It's off the beaten path."

Billy wasn't sure he liked the direction this conversation was headed.

"A good friend is only in town for a couple of nights and I promised I'd hang out with him."

"Him?"

"Yeah."

"Are you involved with him?"

"Yes and no. This'll probably sound awkward, being that we're in the afterglow of butt sex and all"—she flashed him a quick grin—"but you should know that Jon and I have a casual sexual relationship."

Fuck. He asked, "How casual, Eden?" knowing that his tone wasn't casual at all.

"Very. We're good friends, but we're also lovers when the mood strikes us."

A surge of jealousy rocked him so hard that he was surprised his body wasn't convulsing.

"Say something," she demanded.

"I don't know what you want me to say. I've never been in a situation like this."

"Like what?"

"Like my lover asking me to hang out with her other lover."

"Jon and I are friends first." Eden idly stroked the area around his nipple. "Don't you have female friends you've slept with who are still your buddies? Who can fill that need for intimate physical contact once in a while, without strings?"

"No. Truth is, I don't have a ton of friends of either gender. Been too damn busy or I've been on location."

"Well, I think you'll like Jon. He's a great guy."

Billy kissed her nose. "I hope so, since he's my roommate."

"What?"

"I'm assuming you're talking about Jon White Feather, aka Johnny Feather, rock sensation?"

A stunned look crossed her face. "You know him?"

"No. Feather Light owns the condo I'm staying in and Jim White Feather warned me his little brother Jon would be crashing there. I saw his luggage today, but he wasn't around so I haven't met him yet." He trailed his fingers across her collarbone. "And Jim had mentioned you and Jon hooking up whenever he rolled into town."

"Jim just threw that out there in casual conversation?" she said sharply.

"No. I think he didn't want me to be surprised if I saw you wearing Jon's bathrobe or something at the condo." He paused. "Jim doesn't have a clue we knew each other before or that we…"

Eden sighed. "I know Spearfish is a small town and we know some of the same people, but this is just bizarre."

"Tell me about it," he muttered. What were the odds he'd be rooming with the only other person Eden had slept with in the last three years?

"So is that a no for tomorrow night?"

"It sounds like fun."

"Good." She yawned and snuggled into him. "Are you staying over?"

"Do you want me to?"

"I'd like that."

Holding Eden all night? Definitely heaven. His arms tightened around her. "Me too."

Chapter Twelve

THE NEXT EVENING Eden and Jon exited the dance floor and returned to the table where Billy waited. The night was going far better than Eden anticipated. Billy and Jon showed up together, acting like best buds. Apparently they'd spent the morning playing basketball and shooting the shit.

The cocktail waitress swung by and pressed her boobs in Jon's face. "Need anything, darlin'?"

"Sure, I'll take another Coke. What about you guys?"

Billy and Eden shook their heads. After Miss Look At My Tits sashayed away, Eden asked Jon, "You ever get sick of all the female attention?"

Before he could answer, two rhinestone cowgirls approached and demanded a dance. After Jon politely declined, they focused their attention on Billy. When he also declined, they focused their venomous looks on Eden and stomped off.

The single women in this place were hostile. At first she chalked up their attitudes to the fact she, Billy and Jon weren't regulars at the

Silver Star. Then she decided the women were jealous because she was in the company of two great-looking young guys. But she also suspected the sneers and whispers were because she was an Indian woman with two gorgeous guys, one of whom was white.

Putting aside her paranoia, she refocused on the conversation.

"Too bad you're only here temporarily," Jon said. "I know Feather Light needed another full-time engineer before Bob's heart attack."

She listened while Billy launched into a detailed explanation of the other projects he'd been handling.

"The bottom line remains they are swamped. I'm doing what I can while I'm here."

"*Has* Jim said anything to you about staying on permanently?"

Billy shrugged but wouldn't meet Eden's inquisitive gaze. "He's hinted, but I think he's waiting to see how my report on this initial assignment turns out."

Eden swigged her beer and feigned interest in the neon bucking bull above the bar.

A warm hand pressed into the small of her back. Equally warm lips brushed her ear. "Dance with me." Billy tugged her onto the dance floor, holding her against his body with a firm possessiveness that heated her blood.

They swayed together, lost in the rhythm of the music, secure in the synchronicity of their bodies. By the end of the third song, Eden needed a break from the intense feelings Billy aroused with just a simple touch.

She escaped to the bathroom and locked herself in a stall, attempting to regain control of her emotions. Was there a chance Billy would stick around? If so, where did that leave them? Would he be interested in pursuing a relationship with her?

The outer door slammed against the garbage can. An angry female voice whined, "He turned me down again. And that ugly Indian bitch wasn't with him this time."

Eden peeked out the crack in the stall door. The two pesky rhinestone cowgirls from earlier were primping in front of the mirror.

"Give it up, Jackie. So what if he's gorgeous? You can ask him until you're as red in the face as he is and he ain't gonna say yes. Them Indians always stick together."

Her stomach lurched. They were talking about her.

"But it don't make sense the white guy with them said no."

"Why are you surprised? She's probably doin' both of them."

"What the fuck do they see in her? She ain't pretty. Her clothes look like Salvation Army rejects. She's probably always drunk, and dumb as tipi post."

"So she's another fuckin' slutty Indian squaw. Why do you care?"

Eden felt sick and lowered herself to the toilet seat.

"Because they're the best lookin' guys in here tonight."

"They're not the *only* guys. You don't wanna be with a white dude who sticks his dick in red meat anyway."

The bimbos exited in a burst of braying laughter.

Eden cooled her heels until her temper waned, but nothing erased the embarrassment. A couple of cutting remarks and her hard-won confidence disappeared, allowing the pitiable little Indian girl who still lurked inside her to resurface. She slunk from the bathroom, keeping her eyes on the concrete floor until she reached the table.

Jon sat by himself. When he saw her, his smile died and he stood abruptly. "Eden? What's wrong?"

"Where's Billy?"

"Had to take a phone call from his boss in Chicago." Jon cupped her face. "What happened?"

"Same shit, different day." She tried to wriggle out of his hold. "Look. I can't stand to be here. I'm leaving."

"The hell you are. What happened to make you turn tail and run?"

"Nothing." She cringed when the women passed by their table and Jon caught her reaction.

He swore softly. "What did they say to you?"

"It doesn't matter."

"You know you'll feel better if you talk to me." He swept her hair over her shoulder. "You know I'll understand."

"I know. But not here. Please. Let me go."

"Fine." Jon's gaze was laser sharp. "Come to the condo. We'll talk there."

"No. I just want to go home."

"Not a chance. I'll get Billy—"

Eden was near tears. But she'd be damned if she'd give those women the satisfaction. "Just drop it."

"Drop what?" Billy's hands squeezed her shoulders.

"She won't tell me what happened, so let's get out of this redneck dive and head back to the condo." Jon's thumbs stroked her hot cheeks. "You want Billy to drive your car?"

"I'm fine. I need some air. I'll follow you."

Billy's voice tickled her ear. "You sure?"

Eden nodded.

They released her and somehow she made it to her car without bawling.

EDEN FELT RIDICULOUS, seated between the men on the small sofa in the condo, Jon holding one hand, Billy the other, as she told them what'd transpired in the bathroom.

In retrospect, she'd heard worse things, racial slurs barked directly in her face, so she didn't know why she'd gotten so upset and worked up over it this time.

Billy demanded, "Does this bullshit happen often?"

"Yes," she and Jon answered simultaneously.

Thick silence descended.

"Is that why it's easier for you two…to be together?"

Eden looked at Billy oddly. "Indians always stick together?"

"That's not what I meant."

"Love doesn't discriminate about varying skin colors, but everyone else does. Jim's wife Cindy is white. They've been married for almost twenty years and they still get dirty looks and snide comments."

"Same thing with Tate and Nathan LeBeau. She says it's not just white people who are prejudiced. Some Indians claim that's how the whites are conquering their race. By intermarrying and reproducing half-breeds."

"Not like we can do anything about it, either," Jon said. "We're either a social experiment or socially shunned."

"No one needs shit like that. Jesus. People are fucking idiots," Billy muttered.

"It's just another thing to deal with. We poor half-breeds hafta stick together, eh? Especially since our families can be the worst offenders."

"Is that true for you?" Billy asked Eden.

She inhaled and released a long breath. "Yeah. I don't know if you remember me telling you, but my mother got knocked up when she was drunk. She had no idea who my father was and resented me when I came out of the chute looking like an Indian. Or part Indian. Or whatever the hell I am."

"Hey." Jon grabbed her chin in his hand, turning her face to his. "What you are is beautiful." He pressed a soft kiss to her lips.

Billy cleared his throat and Eden's head whipped back to him. But no censure darkened his eyes, just heat. He touched her face exactly as Jon had. "And sexy." His mouth brushed hers and he expanded the kiss from Jon's simple peck.

Two quick tugs on her hair had her facing Jon again. "And smart." Jon licked the seam of her lips until she opened fully and he dove in for a slow tangling of tongues.

Jon's kisses were more practiced than the raw hunger Billy's mouth unleashed. Their tastes were different too—Jon's was exotic, like cinnamon and sage. Billy's was darker and sweeter, like red wine laced with honey. Both were delicious. Both were intoxicating. Both went to her head as fast as a shot of whiskey.

Jon released her mouth and Billy was back for more. "And you're sweet, Eden. You are so damn..." The rest of his response was lost as he inhaled her in a kiss so blistering hot she wondered if her lips would bear scorch marks.

Her senses were overwhelmed. She didn't want to analyze what was happening. She just wanted to exist in the moment. Eden closed her eyes, dropping her head back on the couch cushion when four male hands began caressing her. Her throat. Her breasts. Her thighs. Her body shuddered from their erotic attention.

"Eden? Baby, do you want this?"

"Want what?" she managed.

Billy's breath tickled her ear. "Want both of us."

"At the same time," Jon said, his lips drifting down her neck.

Heat sparked inside her and she moaned.

"Is that a yes?"

She nodded.

"Say the words," Billy insisted. "Tell us what you want so there won't be any misunderstandings."

Could she do this? Have two men at once? Two men not just kissing and petting her, but licking and sucking and expecting the same in return. Two sets of rough male hands touching her everywhere. Two mouths to kiss and bite and suck on her skin, on her sex. Two cocks demanding entrance to her body.

Was she a carbon copy of her mother if she admitted she wanted that sexy scenario as much as her next breath?

No. Billy and Jon weren't some random guys looking for kicks from an easy lay, they were special to her. They'd treat this—and her—as a sexual experience to be celebrated not as just another kinky threesome. They both knew how to make her body weep with want and vibrate with pleasure. She'd be damned if her mother's ghost would ruin something else for her.

"Baby?"

"Yes. I want both of you to fuck me. At the same time. One night of anything goes down and dirty wicked sex."

"Good answer," Billy murmured. "But make no mistake about

who's in charge. You will do whatever we say."

Eden cracked her eyes open. "Have you guys been planning this all day?"

"No. But neither of us is about to let a golden opportunity pass us by, right Billy?"

"Damn straight."

Jon stood and held a hand out. "Come on. Bedroom. Now."

She gripped Billy's hand and allowed Jon to lead them into a room at the end of the hallway.

A bout of nerves surfaced when she saw the bed.

"Relax," Jon said. "Trust us to make you feel as beautiful as you are to us, Eden." His head dipped and he captured her lips. He began to unbutton her blouse. As soon as it hit the carpet, another set of eager hands unhooked her bra and the scrap of lace disappeared.

Then Billy's hot, hard male skin pressed up against her back. He swept her hair aside, nibbling from her left shoulder to her nape.

Her skin became a mass of goose bumps and she trembled.

Eden gasped when Jon tweaked her nipple. He slid his lips free from hers and replaced his fingers with his hungry mouth.

"Oh. God."

"Do you know how fucking hot it is to watch him sucking on your tits?"

"Help him. I want to feel both your mouths on my breasts at the same time."

Billy growled at her request and moved in front of her. He watched her face as his abrasive tongue lapped the pebbled tip. The same motion in the same spot. Over and over.

Jon mirrored Billy's actions. Tiny flicks of a tongue. Suckling the point with pursed lips. Blowing a soft stream of air across the wetness. Drawing as much of her breast into the wet heat as possible, sucking long and deep and hard.

She'd never experienced anything so visually and physically arousing. Jon's dark head on one side, Billy's blond head on the other. The sensations of each hungry mouth focused solely on her nipple, the same, yet different.

The sharp dual nip of teeth made her cry out. A hot burst of moisture soaked her panties.

"Get her goddamn pants off," Billy said.

Zip. The denim pooled around her ankles. She kicked the jeans away. Keeping his smoldering eyes on hers, Billy knelt and oh-so-slowly dragged the lace underwear down her legs.

A wave of heat nearly buckled her knees.

"On the bed."

Eden scooted into the middle and propped herself on her elbows to see both men undress without a striptease. Not that she complained. She didn't want to wait for all that gorgeous, male flesh that was hers for the taking.

"Toss me a pillow," Billy said. He tapped Eden's ass and she lifted her hips. "Spread those legs wide. I want to see every inch of that pussy."

Jon swept the pad of his thumb across her lower lip. "You ready to have my cock in your mouth?"

She nodded.

"Jon, do you have something we can bind her hands with?"

Holy crap. "But—"

Then Billy was right in her face. "But nothing. You agreed to being with both of us, which means you are ours to do with as we please. And it'd please me greatly to see you tied up and at my mercy."

Three bandanas appeared. Two were looped around her wrists; the third was used to tie her bound hands to the iron slats in the headboard.

It was hot as hell, seeing the lustful sexual greed on Jon and Billy's faces. The inside of her thighs were drenched. Her skin was so hot she feared she'd inadvertently set the cotton sheets on fire.

Jon straddled her chest on his knees. He braced one hand on the headboard and used the other to grip his cock as he circled the mushroomed head over her lips. "Lick it."

Her tongue darted out to swipe the bead leaking from the slit. Another pearly drop appeared and she licked it too.

"That's good. Now open up, dollface."

Eden's lips parted and Jon fed his cock into her mouth, past her teeth, over her tongue until the tip poked the back of her throat. When her lips tightened around his considerable girth and she swallowed, Jon groaned.

"Gonna fuck this sassy mouth." He pulled out and pushed back in, each stroke more insistent. "Suck harder. Like that."

When Billy dragged his tongue from her hole to her clit, she arched up, moaning around Jon's rigid cock.

"Jesus. You're so fucking wet I feel like I'm bathing in you." Billy burrowed his tongue into her slick channel, licking the juices from the inside out.

She bumped her hips higher, desperate for contact on her clit, but he allowed her no control. He held her hips down and fucked her pussy with his tongue.

The pace of Jon's rigid cock slamming into her mouth increased.

He shoved one last time, staying balls deep as his cock twitched and jerked on her tongue.

Thick, warm ejaculate coated her throat and she swallowed repeatedly even as his hips continued to pump into her face.

Jon stilled and glanced down; his blue eyes glittered triumphantly. With his cock still buried in her mouth, he tenderly stroked her cheek with his knuckles. "Eden. You're beautiful. Honest to God beautiful from the inside out. Don't ever forget that. Don't ever let anyone make you feel less than you are." He pushed off the headboard and slipped from between her lips.

But Eden didn't have time to bask in Jon's compliments. Billy zigzagged the flickering end of his tongue up her labia and demanded, "Fly apart for me."

Then he suctioned his mouth to her clit and tongued her relentlessly, imprisoning her hips as she bucked and thrashed. The rush of blood to the sensitive nub wasn't a slow, sweet throbbing, but a tidal wave of epic proportions. One second she was floating toward heaven, the next she was sobbing Billy's name in the maelstrom of pure sensation.

After she'd descended back to earth from the sexual high, Billy untied her hands. She couldn't help but notice his cock was still hard as a club. How'd that happen? Jon had gotten off. She'd gotten off. But Billy hadn't.

Billy's heavy-lidded gaze locked to hers as he gently rubbed the red marks on her wrists. "My turn. On your knees on the floor. Now."

She scooted off the bed, parking herself between Billy's outstretched legs. It didn't matter she'd just finished blowing Jon; she ached to wring the same explosion from Billy. To experience that rush of erotic power when he gripped her head, thrust deep and detonated his male essence in her mouth. To see his sated expression and feel smug she'd taken him there.

Eden bent forward and licked the thick vein pulsing up the center of Billy's cock and suckled his purple cockhead.

"That feels good but that's not what I have in mind."

"Then what?"

Billy picked up her hand and circled it around the base of his stiff cock. "I want your mouth on my nipples while you jack me off, Eden."

That was blunt. But sexy as all get out.

With deliberate sensuality, Billy's fingertips created a path of fire from the upper swell of her breast to the tip of her nipple. "Then I'm going to come on your tits. There's something very appealing about marking you with my seed."

Everything in her that'd been pliant and sated went hot, tight, wet and wanting.

"Watching that'll make me hard again," Jon said.

"Come on, baby. Give Jon a real show. He's a showman. He'll appreciate it. But not as much as I will." Billy knotted his hand in her hair and tugged her to his right nipple.

Eden pursed her swollen lips over the flat disk and began to suck softly. After several attempts of trying to work his cock, she realized the angle was wrong. She stood, propped two fluffy pillows beneath her knees and yanked Billy's slender hips down so he was barely balanced on his elbows on the edge of the bed.

"Mmm. That's better. Need a little lube, though." Rather than use the tube of K-Y on the bed, she reached between her legs, getting her hand wet from her juices. Then she wrapped her fingers around

Billy's cock again and pumped from root to tip.

Behind her, Jon groaned. "Fuck. That's hot as hell, Eden."

Billy's response was an unintelligible male grunt.

Smiling, she nipped at the flat disks and began to vigorously stroke that beautifully hard prick. No slow build up. No tease and retreat. She jacked him faster and faster. Biting and licking and sucking his nipples. Appreciating his groans. Loving the taste of his sweat and need. Relishing the feel of his hips pumping up to meet her strokes.

"Jesus. Fuck." Billy knocked her hand away from his cock and clamped his palm on her shoulder, holding her in place. He pumped frantically as long streams of come jetted out the end of his cock and splashed on her breasts. His eyes were wild blue flames and he growled as spurt after spurt dotted her chest. Pure animal satisfaction was etched on Billy's face as he stared at the milky liquid dripping off her nipples.

Her pussy was sopping wet again. As her sex clenched and throbbed, she squeezed her thighs together and gasped when a tiny orgasm rocked her. She looked up and saw Billy's eyes were still on fire, still devouring her.

"Jesus you're beautiful. Absolutely steal-my-fucking-breath beautiful, Eden."

Her heart damn near turned over in her chest.

He released her shoulder and his hand moved down to cup the underswell of her left breast. His thumb brushed a thick rivulet of come from the tip of her nipple and he brought it to her lips.

Eden opened her mouth and sucked his thumb inside, swirling her tongue, savoring his taste.

"Again." Billy dragged his finger through the sticky wetness cooling on her breast and held the offering to her.

Eyes on his, she licked away every drop.

They made it through two more rounds of erotic finger painting before Jon said brusquely, "Enough. It's my turn and after that little display I'm hard enough I could fuck her clear through the wall." Jon helped Eden to her feet and wiped away the remnants of Billy's spent passion.

She shivered at the cool washcloth skating over her heated skin, wondering when Jon had left the room. No surprise neither she nor Billy noticed.

"Eden." Jon's melodic voice tickled her ear and she trembled.

"What?"

He didn't answer immediately, he lazily traced every vertebrae down her spine, causing the buzzing sensation in her skin to hum back to life. She'd never experienced arousal this prolonged. Never believed she could ache for more.

"I want you." Jon's teeth sank into the slope of her shoulder and she cried out from the pleasurable nip of pain. His next words and his hot breath burned her like a brand. "But I want to tie you up first."

"Why?"

"Not only do I get off thinking about fucking you as deep and as long as I want, but it's a way for you to give yourself over to us, before we take you completely." He clasped her hands together behind her back, twisting the bandanas around her wrists again. Then he gently spun her around. "Close your eyes."

Eden feared she might topple over from too much stimulation on her sex organs and not enough blood reaching her brain.

Soft lips drifted down her jawline, starting on the left side below her earlobe, ending at the right. Those sweetly arousing lips traveled up her hairline from her temple across her forehead and down the left side. Then Jon rained kisses on her eyelids. Her cheekbones. The corners of her mouth before taking her mouth in a wet, sizzling kiss that robbed her lungs of air and her mind of reason.

"On the bed." Jon crawled on first and stretched out on his back. He rolled on a condom and looked at Billy. "Help her. She's going to be facing you as she's riding me."

Anticipation quickened her pulse. Without use of her hands it was difficult to balance, but Billy steadied her, helping her straddle Jon's pelvis.

"Your knees need to be wider."

Eden shot him a panicked look over her shoulder. "But I'll fall forward."

Jon smacked her ass and she yelped. "No, you won't. I'll be holding your hips. Now spread 'em."

Billy braced her shoulders as she lowered on Jon's cock.

"Oh yeah, you're really wet." He guided his shaft inside her to the hilt and stilled all movement. His hands floated up her bound arms. "You okay?"

"Yeah."

"Slow and easy. Let Billy tend to you while I enjoy your beautiful body and prep you to take both of us."

Her eyes were focused on Billy as Jon began to rock his hips. The movement was subtle but accurate. The widest portion of his cockhead continually pressed her G-spot.

"Oh. That's good." She gasped. "Really good."

Billy caught her next gasp in his mouth. His tongue speared past her lips, languidly dueling with hers. His hand stretched from her collarbone and curled around her neck, holding her in place. He flattened his other hand and it drifted down her quivering belly. The long middle finger reached her bikini line and kept going until the tip connected with her clit. He rubbed tiny circles and more wetness flooded her pussy.

Jon fucked her in a steady rocking motion. His hands roved from her calves to her arms to the crack of her ass in a constant caress. "So beautiful. Every part of you."

She was teetering on the edge of complete meltdown. Jon controlled her sex and the movement of her hips; Billy controlled her mouth and her clit.

And her heart.

No time for that emotional detour now.

Concentrate on nothing but physical pleasure and the pulsing, throbbing, sexual adoration these men are bestowing on you.

Billy put his mouth on her ear. "It's right there, Eden." He increased the pace of his stroking finger. "Scream, baby. Come for me. Come for Jon."

Just like that, her body erupted. She cried out as her clit spasmed and her internal muscles clamped down on Jon's cock like a vise. Surge after surge bombarded her.

When the throbs became little pulses, Billy licked the sweat running down her throat, latched onto the sweet spot on her neck with his mouth and sucked, shooting her into orbit again. "Oh God, oh God, oh God, stop. I can't take any more."

"Ssh. Baby, it's okay. I've got you."

Breath sawed in and out of her mouth. She had to rely on Billy to keep her upright. "Please."

"Eden. Look at me." He tilted her chin up and she blinked her eyes open. "I need you to turn around so Jon and I can take you together, okay?"

"But—"

"This is what you wanted."

You're what I wanted. You're all I ever wanted.

Why couldn't he see that?

And just for a moment, she thought he did realize it when he murmured, "Trust us. Trust me. This is a one time only wicked, wild thing, remember?"

Jon untied her hands and massaged her wrists. He patted her ass and she lifted on her knees, letting his still hard erection slip free from her sheath. Then Eden threw her leg over Jon's hip and faced him.

His grin was pure conquering warrior. "I apologize in advance. This ain't gonna last long, because I'm about to blow."

"You don't have to prove your staying power to me. You've wrung me out."

Plastic crinkled behind her as Billy donned a condom.

Jon gathered her against his chest and kissed her. Keeping her focus on the soft, wet, warm recess of his mouth as Billy coated her puckered hole with cool gel.

Eden shuddered with want when Billy inserted one slippery finger past the ring of muscles. More gel, another finger coating her, stretching her. Fucking her. Marking her.

"So tight. So hot. So *mine.*" Fingers were replaced with the head of his cock. "Gonna be good, but baby, it'll be hard and short."

"Such an adventurous girl, taking us both on. How's it gonna feel to be stuffed with cock?" Jon cranked her head to the side and sucked the sensitive skin above her collarbone, ratcheting her need another level.

A tickling tongue zigzagged up her spine. "Ready?" Billy breathed against the back of her head.

"Past ready. Do it now."

Billy canted her pelvis to his liking. Jon reached between their bodies, poising his cock at the entrance to her pussy.

They plunged into her simultaneously.

"Oh God." She felt every twitch and jerk of their cocks in her ass and her pussy and her womb, even when they weren't moving.

Billy stayed in place while Jon pulled out. Then they switched. Back and forth. Their bodies shook uncontrollably, yet they kept an easy, careful penetration. But that wasn't what Eden wanted. She wanted roughness, no-holds-barred passion. To be used shamelessly. "Stop."

Both men froze. Jon said, "Are we hurting you?"

"No. I want you to let loose. I want you guys to fuck me like you mean it." She tightened her anus and her pussy around their cocks and they both hissed. "I won't break." She turned her head and challenged Billy. "But I dare you to try."

Billy snarled, "You asked for it," and rammed deep.

Jon twisted his fingers in her hair and jerked her head up so he could watch his cock impaling her. Over and over.

They fucked her without pause. Thrusting together. Each taking what they needed. Sandwiched between slick, hard, pounding bodies, surrounded by the scents of sex and the sound of primal male grunts, she started to come apart with a prolonged scream of complete female satisfaction, taking both men over the edge with her.

No one said a word.

Billy pulled out first and left the room. She rolled off Jon, landing flat on her back on the mattress. Several seconds passed as she acclimated her breathing.

Then Jon's serious face was above hers. "You're beautiful. Thank you for sharing yourself with me one last time."

"Oh, I see. Now that you've proven your rock star penchant for threesomes, you're tossing me out?"

"No." He pushed a section of hair behind her ear. "I'm stepping aside."

"What?"

"We're still friends, great friends, but no more friends with bennies. Billy is a great guy and he really cares about you."

"How do you know?"

"Any man who'd willingly share his woman with another man because that's what she wanted, even when it makes him see red, is a man insanely in love."

"But—"

"No buts. Trust in it. Trust in him. Be happy, dollface. You deserve it." He kissed her forehead. Like a friend would. "Now scram. I need my beauty sleep."

Eden hopped off the bed and dressed, noticing Billy's clothes were already gone.

Chapter Thirteen

Billy heard her footsteps coming down the hall and wondered how he should play this. Knowing Eden, ignoring it was his best option.

He faced her. "Hey, beautiful. You okay?"

"Yeah. Worn out. I should go."

No. Stay. He smiled tightly. "I'll walk you out." It surprised him when she reached for his hand as they left the condo and walked to her car.

Cicadas sang in the trees, filling the silence.

Finally she spoke. "Can I ask you something?"

"Sure."

"Are you done with the Feather Light project?"

"Almost."

"What happens now?"

"I'll have a final decision by tomorrow." Feeling helpless, he let go of her and shoved his hands in his jeans. "You know I have to give the city my recommendation first?"

She nodded and glanced away.

But not before he caught her hopeless look. Were her eyes tearing up? Or was that a trick of the moonlight? His stomach muscles knotted. "Come over for dinner tomorrow night."

Her suspicious gaze whipped back to him. "You cook?"

"No. But I do a mean take-out order. It'll give us some time alone before—"

"—you go back to Chicago."

"Does it bother you? The thought of me leaving?"

"It doesn't surprise me." After opening the SUV door, she stopped. "Good luck with your reports. Call me tomorrow and let me know what time I should come over."

"Eden—"

"Goodnight, Billy." The door clicked shut. She started the engine, the radio blared Stone Temple Pilots and she sped off.

"That went well," he said to her taillights.

SEVERAL HOURS LATER Billy rubbed the grit from his eyes. Decision made, he signed off on the report, printed two copies and hastily shoved the sheaf of papers on top of the desk in the living room.

He'd drop off the original tomorrow. Maybe put it off until the next day if it'd give him more time with Eden. He crawled in bed, unsure for the first time in his career whether he'd made the best choice.

The white ceiling wasn't particularly interesting, but he stared at it for an eternity before he drifted into an uneasy sleep.

EARLY THE NEXT evening Billy made one last visual sweep of the setting. Timer set so the food didn't dry out. Candles lit. Music playing. Wine uncorked. He expelled a nervous sigh. How would Eden react to his confession? Especially after he told her he had to leave first thing in the morning? *Hey, I love you, but I gotta go.*

The doorbell dinged.

Eden slunk in wearing a skin-tight black cat suit and a cat-like grin. "Hope I'm not too early."

Billy wrapped his hand around her neck and took her mouth. The taste of her burst on his tongue. "Might be a little early for dessert."

"Mmm." Her dainty fingertips traced a straight line from his throat to his stomach, lingering on the waistband of his jeans. "I was thinking more along the lines of an appetizer." On tiptoes, she brushed a fleeting kiss on his chin. "But I guess I can wait for dessert, if you can." She sauntered to the breakfast bar separating the small kitchen and the living area.

Damn. He drooled at the curve of her ass and followed her like a dog on a leash. He'd need every ounce of patience to survive the night. While he poured the wine, she silently assessed the condo's sparse furnishings.

"What's your apartment like in Chicago?"

"A lot like this." Boring. Bland. Lonely. "Although it does have a better view."

Eden murmured her thanks when he passed her a glass of red wine. "You've made your decision?"

"Yes. But you know I can't tell you—"

"I know." A beat passed, then two. "I am anxious, but mostly because I'm not sure *what* I want anymore."

"Professionally?"

"And personally."

If he said the wrong thing she'd clam up. He kept his tone off-hand. "Well, you already own a charming bungalow with the picket fence. Looking for a husband and the 2.5 kids to go along with it?"

"I have three hundred kids right now who count on me," she said dryly. "It's a pretty hefty responsibility. Besides, I can't imagine with my upbringing that I'd have any parenting skills." She poured merlot in her empty glass. "I've focused all my energies at the center. I don't have time for much else. Didn't you say your social life was pathetic? Mine is worse. My friends are more forgiving than the men who've tried to have a relationship with me."

"Which is why hooking up with Jon works out?"

"Yeah. We've been buddies since college. No chance either of us wants more." She smiled. "Last night was unbelievably hot."

"No regrets?"

"No. But it's not an experience I ever have to repeat. Guess I'm more of a one-woman man."

He'd be that man if he had anything to say about it. "So, if you've been hooking up with Jon whenever the mood strikes you, when was your last actual relationship?"

"Three years ago."

"How long did it last?"

Eden's eyes narrowed. "How long did *your* most recent relationship last, Billy?"

"The longest relationship I've ever had lasted a month."

She truly looked shocked. "So what is wrong with us?"

"Maybe we're not willing to settle for second best when we've had the real thing."

"Real? Lord. We were so young neither of us knew what that meant."

Billy angled across the counter and briefly placed his mouth over hers. "I know you don't want to talk about this. But what we had ten years ago was real."

The timer on the stove dinged. *Saved by the bell.* Billy dropped the discussion. "Come on. Let's eat."

During dinner Eden was as animated, slyly sarcastic and charming as ever. After they'd devoured the meal, she washed the dishes while he dried. Peace settled over him. What would it be like to come home to her every night? While her hands were occupied, he snugged his body behind hers, holding aside her silky hair so he could trail warm kisses down her neck.

She angled her head letting him take what he wanted.

"Coffee?" he murmured.

"No. I'm too wired the way it is."

"Why?"

"Partially because you've made the decision regarding the center and you're so damn good at hiding it. Partially because I'm anxious to be with you all sweaty and naked in the dark."

He chuckled. "Soon. But I have a surprise for you first, so why don't you make yourself comfortable in the living room?"

She spun around and placed a soapy hand over his heart. "Billy, you didn't have to go to all this trouble."

"I know. I wanted to." He'd meant to say something witty, but the seriousness in the tawny depths of her eyes changed his mind. "I can't think for wanting you. Just you." His mouth met hers in a sweet, slow, bone-melting kiss. "Go sit down before I forget my own damn name."

She turned on her high heel and left him gawking after her like a tongue-tied boy.

Once Billy regained control, he removed the box from the fridge and dimmed the lights in the living room.

Eden was tucked in the corner of the white leather couch. She looked so small, so wary. So damn perfect his heart nearly stopped.

He handed her the clear plastic box. "This is for you."

A beat passed. "That's exactly like the corsage you gave me for prom."

"I know. Remember you threw it at my head when I took off?"

"Pretty childish, huh?"

"No. It was childish I left without explaining why."

Eden's lower lip trembled before she firmed it. "I can't believe you remembered."

"I can't believe you'd think I'd forget." Billy helped her to her feet and slipped the corsage from the package. The heavy scent of gardenia filled the room. Eden held out her wrist, he slid the stretchy silver band over her small hand.

An eternity passed as she fingered the white roses surrounding the creamy gardenia. She lifted the corsage and inhaled. "Why?"

"To show you I've never forgotten you. Leaving you is the only thing in my life I regret. Can we go back in time, just for tonight and be those two people who were so crazy for each other?"

EDEN FOUGHT A wave of tears. Dammit. She should tell Billy the truth. She wanted him the way he was *now*—the gentle, thrilling, demanding man he'd become and not the confused young man he'd been.

Before the end of the night she'd tell Billy how she felt about him. Before she found out his decision on the community center. Before she lost her nerve and let him walk out of her life again. "I'm still crazy about you, Billy."

"Show me."

His gentle caresses turned energetic. Mouths, which had teased with slow, deep, wet kisses, became frantic. When Billy pulled his lips away, Eden whimpered and tried to reconnect their hunger.

"No. I want to do this right. We have all the time in the world." He opened his hot mouth on the tender skin beneath her jaw line and sucked.

She allowed him this fantasy and repeated the words she'd said that night at the Motel 6. "Make love to me."

Billy studied her face, his blue eyes filled with longing. Slowly, too slowly, his deft fingers peeled the silky material off her shoulders and down her arms. Breathing unevenly, his hands clenched on her hips, he merely stared at her.

Her skin tightened, spreading the aching, needy feeling throughout her body. "You gonna gawk at me all night?"

"Maybe." He tugged until her one-piece outfit slithered to the carpet. Clad in black bikini panties and a black demi-bra, she shifted on the knee-high spike-heeled black leather boots and kicked her clothes away.

"Should I call you 'Mistress Eden' in that get-up?" One blunt finger traveled from the hollow of her throat to the dip in her navel, sending waves of heat rippling across her skin. "Or should I ask if you have a cat-o'-nine tails hidden in your purse?"

"Seems you're well-acquainted with pleasure tools. Got some bondage fantasies, Mr. Buchanan?" she murmured silkily.

"Only with you. Next time, leave the boots on, but for now, take them off. I want to feel nothing except your skin on mine."

Eden sensed Billy's control had stretched to a thin line. She sought to shatter it.

She swiveled her hips, bracing her hands on the back of the couch. With her back flattened, her ass curved up in blatant enticement. Exposing the dampness between her thighs was like waving a red flag in front of a bull, but she did it anyway. Glancing over her shoulder, she wet her lips. "A little help removing the boots? I'm having a hard time catching my balance."

"I'm having a hard time catching my breath." Next thing she knew, Billy slung her over his shoulder in a fireman's hold and was striding to the bedroom like his feet were on fire.

She squealed, "Billy!" when he sharply smacked her ass.

"You definitely need to learn submission." He set her on the bed and yanked her boots off. Darkness disappeared as he lit the candles lined up on the nightstand.

She melted as easily as candle wax when faced with his romantic side. "Maybe I'm dominant. I like being on top."

"You'll get your chance later. For now," he started to unbutton his dress shirt, "you get to be on the bottom."

Soon as he was naked, Billy swept the bedding to the floor. He eased her panties off, unhooked her bra. In one graceful move he slid her to the center of the mattress, her underneath him.

The coolness of the cotton sheets on her back exaggerated the feverish feeling of his heated skin on hers. She couldn't help the small shudder of anticipation.

"Cold?" he asked, smoothing tangles of hair away from her face.

She shook her head.

His hand looked enormous drifting down her body, so capable of exacting pleasure as it skimmed over her beaded nipples, past the indent of her navel to disappear between her legs.

Her breath caught.

Billy didn't stop his indolent caresses as he pressed his lips to the delicate skin below her ear. His middle finger slid inside her sheath. He made circles inside her, lazily licking down her throat. "I want you nice and wet. Open and ready for me."

Eden wriggled her hips higher to meet his rhythmic strokes when he added another finger. With a hint of steel in her voice she clamped down on her internal muscles, trying to pull his fingers deeper and said, "I am ready."

"Not yet."

With his continual attention to her clit, an orgasm rocketed through her. She moaned his name as every region of her pelvis contracted in pulsing billows that didn't end until he gently withdrew his hand.

A condom package rustled. Billy spread her thighs wide.

"Eden. Look at me."

She focused on those serious blue eyes as his body covered hers.

The scent of Billy, vanilla candles and sweet flowers surrounded her, making her dizzy. "You're smashing my corsage."

"Forget it." Billy's hips pressed forward and he slipped just the head into her opening. "The only thing I want you thinking about is me." He kissed her. "About us." He kissed her again, longer, sweeter. "How if we'd done this years ago I wouldn't have had the guts to leave you." He thrust inside her completely.

Their joining was as tangled as Eden's emotions, fierce one minute, tender the next. And when neither could hold back any longer, he whispered, "With me, Eden, always with me."

They came together in a molten rush.

As she lay crushed beneath Billy's spent body and the weight of his words, she knew losing her job paled in comparison to losing this man.

Chapter Fourteen

BILLY SNORED LIKE a damn freight train.

At first, Eden was amused by the escalating snuffles. With his arm firmly wrapped around her waist and her body tucked against his, she couldn't move and she couldn't get back to sleep. She lifted his arm and rolled away, hastily jamming the pillow in her empty spot.

Billy didn't notice.

She snagged his shirt off the floor and buttoned up while creeping from the room.

Moonlight beamed through the skylight in the hallway. The ceiling fan above the dining room table whirred softly and the refrigerator quietly hummed. A shiver broke free when her bare feet hit the cold kitchen tile.

It was weird, wandering through the condo alone in the dark, knowing Billy was as much a stranger in this place as she was. A tickle in her throat reminded her she'd worked up quite a thirst. She plucked a wine glass from the dish rack, turned the faucet on low and gulped three cold glasses before the dryness disappeared.

Eden rested her backside on the counter. The digital clock on the microwave read one-fifteen. They'd been in bed roughly four hours.

Every single time he'd touched her had been different tonight, urgent, sweet, raunchy. He'd been amazingly attuned to her needs just by looking into her eyes. She was half-afraid the man knew she'd fallen in love with him again.

Again? Why won't you admit Billy has always had your heart?

She meandered into the sparsely furnished living room, too keyed up to sleep. No magazines littered the coffee table. The shelves held not one paperback book. She fought the urge to flee, yet she didn't want to skulk away without so much as a *thank you for the orgasms*. Plus, she did have that whole confessing her love for him thing to get through.

A single window separated the living and dining areas. She skirted the small desk, pulled back the heavy curtain and stared outside, watching the moonbeams throw shadows across the pavement.

As she turned away in the darkness, her thigh bumped the desk, scattering stacks of papers and file folders. Eden muffled a curse, set down her water glass and tried to straighten the piles.

That's when she saw an envelope addressed to the City of Spearfish.

Her stomach dropped to her toes. The contents of that flimsy envelope held her future.

Then she noticed something else: the envelope hadn't been sealed.

Did that mean Billy wasn't certain of his decision?

No. Billy was completely confident where his career was concerned. Still, the open flap stuck out like a sore thumb.

Or a dare.

She reached out and touched the stiff paper, then dropped her hand as if it'd been burned. She really shouldn't. No. She *couldn't*. Peeking would be wrong. Unethical. A breach of trust. If he ever found out…

But the devil on her shoulder reminded her Billy was in the other room making noise which put a chainsaw to shame.

Eden gnawed her lip, racked with indecision.

The jangle of her cell phone broke the eerie silence.

Her gaze encompassed the room as she tried to remember where she'd stashed her purse. She followed the sound to the far corner of the couch. By the time she dug out the phone, it'd stopped ringing.

The blue light glowed as she scrolled through the messages. Ten messages? In the last hour? All from Shelby?

Why would Shelby call her ten times?

She dialed Shelby's cell number. Shelby answered on the second ring. "Eden? Thank God! Where are you? I've been trying to reach you for over an hour."

"Why?" In the background, Eden heard sirens, the squawk of police radios and people shouting. She felt the first stirrings of real panic. "What's up?"

All sound stopped. For a second Eden was afraid they'd lost the connection. Then, in a normal decibel range, Shelby said, "I'm in a police car now so I can hear you."

"Shelby, what the hell is going on?"

"I'm outside the community center. You'd better get here fast."

After hearing Shelby's next words, Eden swayed and dropped to her knees on the carpet. "When? No. I'm okay," she lied. "Of course. I'll be right there."

Dazed, she snapped the phone shut.

"Eden? Baby, what's wrong?"

How long had Billy been standing there? In shock, she just stared at him. Through him. She couldn't seem to make her legs work.

Billy crossed the room. "What is going on?"

"Seems your concerns about the electrical system were dead on. The community center is on fire."

He hauled her to her feet and held her.

Eden dug her nails into the bare skin of his shoulder blades. "Oh God." Another horrifying thought jarred her. "What if Thomas snuck in and spent the night?" Hurriedly she redialed Shelby's number and relayed the information about the young boy. She shut the cell phone with a snap and looked up.

"Come on." Billy ushered her toward the bedroom. "Get dressed and we'll go."

EDEN STARED MINDLESSLY out the window of her car as Billy drove. She'd called Shelby to relay the information the building might've been occupied.

Seemed to take forever to reach the center. Fire trucks and police cars clogged the side streets after blocking off Main Street. When Eden saw the flames licking fifty feet into the air, she bailed out of the car and ran.

She stopped and gaped at the broken shell. The windows had blown out. The roof completely collapsed. The brick interior walls were charred black. Smoke billowed and curled into the cool night air. She gripped the barricade and watched the firefighters lugging equipment. Cops trying to get control of the growing crowd. But her gaze kept returning to the burning building.

Desolation took root and settled deep, increasing that sick feeling.

"Eden?"

A large hand jostled her shoulder and she looked up into the grim face of Detective Danley.

"I'm so sorry. The fire department got here as soon as they could but it was already too late."

Was he talking about Thomas? She swallowed hard. "Did they find him?"

A frown creased the Detective's brow. "Find who?"

"Thomas Fast Wolf. A twelve-year old boy who sometimes sneaks in and sleeps here. He has family problems…" Tears blurred her vision. Images of sweet Thomas danced in her head until she wanted to throw up.

"Eden!" Shelby trotted up and hugged her.

She was too numb to move. The detective pulled Shelby aside and they conversed in low tones. Eden didn't bother to listen; her heart was so heavy with grief she thought she'd collapse beneath the weight of it.

Shelby returned and shook her. "Listen to me. Thomas isn't in there."

Eden blinked at Shelby. "What?"

"After you called me I called Nathan LeBeau. He's had some

dealings with Thomas's parents so he drove over and checked the Fast Wolf house." Shelby grabbed her hands. "Thomas is home. He's been there all night."

Immediately, Eden began to cry.

Shelby hugged her again. "It's just a building. No one was hurt, that's the important thing, right?"

People started to gather around her and offer support. The community outpouring stunned her, but with nothing left but a burned out skeleton, there was no doubt the direction the city would take with the community center.

Finally at about four, the blaze was under control; there was nothing left to burn.

Exhausted, Eden looked around for Billy. Several times in the last few hours she'd wanted him by her side, needing his quiet strength. Wishful thinking because he couldn't have offered it in front of all these people anyway.

As she wound her way through the emergency vehicles, Billy stepped out of the shadows.

Tempting to throw herself into his arms and damn the consequences. Did it really matter if these people knew she needed Billy Buchanan? So what if the mayor and the whole city council saw them? Billy's report wouldn't matter now. Her job was history.

Billy kept his gaze trained on the building. "I overheard the firemen talking. They think it was a gas leak since it spread so fast. Not the electrical system after all."

So cold. So clinical. Eden's hope shriveled and died. He'd already reset the distance between them. His job, his time in Spearfish was done. She wanted to cry but she found she didn't have any tears left.

"You okay?" he asked, finally looking at her.

"Not really." Eden exhaled the breath she'd been holding. "I can't believe it's gone. Makes your job easier, doesn't it?"

"Eden—"

"I suppose you'll be heading back to Chicago sooner than expected?"

Billy's mouth stayed unsmiling, his tone flat. "Actually, I'm leaving tomorrow."

The sweet, romantic night she'd spent in his arms meant nothing? It'd been his way of saying goodbye? "I'm sure you'll be glad to get back. It appears your time here was wasted."

"Wasted? What the hell are you talking about?"

Eden gathered her courage even as her heart shattered. "I saw your recommendation letter to the City Council."

"When?" he demanded.

"Tonight. At the condo. When you were sleeping."

Although she hadn't read the document, by the expression on his face, she knew what his final recommendation had been.

Billy exploded. "For Christ's sake—"

"Don't you dare yell at her." Shelby bulled her way between them. "Leave her alone, Mr. Buchanan."

"You stay out of this."

"No. I've watched you waltz around the community center, charming her, getting her to trust you. She's lost enough tonight without losing her pride, too."

Billy reared back as if he'd been slapped.

As Shelby herded Eden to her car, Eden discovered she had more tears left after all.

Chapter Fifteen

One week later…

EDEN SHOVED THE box in the backseat and slammed the door. "That's the last of it."

"Thanks. I don't know what I would've done without you. You've been the best boss I've ever had." Shelby launched herself into Eden's arms and sobbed.

"Hey. We promised no crying, remember?"

Shelby sniffled. "I'm gonna miss you, though."

"I'll miss you, too."

She shuffled back and straightened Eden's collar. "Promise you'll email me and let me know what's going on?"

"Scouts honor." They wandered through the piles of boxes spread out on Eden's driveway.

A black Ford F150 pickup pulled up to the curb and parked.

"A friend of yours?" she asked Shelby.

Shelby fidgeted beside her Grand Am, strangely hesitant. "No. Yours?"

"No." Who could it be? Then Billy jumped from the cab.

Holy crap. What was he doing here?

Shelby moved in front of her. "You want me to stay?"

Eden murmured, "No. I'll be okay." What a lie. She'd been an absolute mess since Billy left, just like ten years ago. If she thought she'd been hurt then, it was nothing compared to the total annihilation she'd experienced the night of the fire.

Tires squealed as Shelby roared away.

Billy stalked toward her. Did he have to look like he didn't have a care in the world?

"What the hell is this?" He gestured to the boxes. "You going somewhere? I've been trying to call you, going crazy because you never answer."

Maybe he wasn't as blasé as she'd first believed. Deep lines marred his handsome face, along with a scruffy beard. "Hello to you too, Billy."

He stared at her. His eyes roved over every inch of her face. "Sorry. I-I—" He scrubbed his hands over the stubble darkening his chin. "Are these your boxes?"

"Yes."

"Then you are leaving town," he said flatly.

His anger surprised her. Why did he care? A sliver of hope unfurled and she called herself every kind of fool. "I haven't decided what I'm going to do. These boxes were for Shelby. She can't wait around for the new community center to open, so she's taking a job in Cheyenne with her cousin."

A profound look of relief crossed his face. "Thank God." Billy hauled her against his body, locked his mouth to hers and kissed the daylights out of her.

She pushed him away. "Stop. What are you doing here?"

"I'm here for you. For us."

"What? But you left."

"For a lousy week. If you would've let me explain…" Billy imprisoned her head between his hands forcing her to meet his eyes. "I had to go back to Chicago and hand in my resignation in person. So, I have a few things to say to you and you'll damn well listen. No interrupting."

"I don't interrupt."

He lifted a brow.

"Okay," Eden said, "so maybe I do."

Billy smiled and some of the tension in his eyes vanished. "First off, you never read my recommendation to the council or you'd have known I'd urged them to keep the community center right where it was."

Shock had her jaw dropping. "You did?"

"Yes. And second, maybe if you weren't so damn determined to think the worst of me, scared that I'm always going to leave you, you'd realize that I love you and I'm not going anywhere this time."

Tears stung her eyes; she was too stunned to interrupt.

"I'd planned on telling you the night of the fire." He brushed the wetness from her face. "Truth is, I've never stopped caring about you. It took being with you again to drive the point home. So maybe I was young and stupid and we've wasted ten years, but we have lots of years left ahead of us. I think we can make it work. I want to try."

"Me too."

"Good. Because Robert and Jim asked me if I wanted to buy into Feather Light as a partner."

"What did you say?"

"Yes, immediately, before they changed their minds." Billy pressed his forehead to hers. "When I came back here, I saw you've built a support network of friends who've become your family. I want to set down roots with you. Be part of a community. I want a life with you, Eden."

When she didn't speak or move, Billy moved back so he could peer at her. "Say something."

"You told me not to interrupt."

"Smart-ass. Please. Talk. Yell. I don't care. Your silence is killing me."

Eden let her finger trace the worry lines by his eyes. He looked so vulnerable, so unsure of her reaction it made her ache inside. "Oh God, Billy, I'm so in love with you—"

His lips slid over hers in a gentle kiss as tears fell freely from her eyes. "Say it again," he whispered against her mouth. "I feel like I've been waiting my whole life to hear you say it."

"I love you. I've always loved you. I wanted to die when you took off for Chicago, even when I planned to track you down and kick your ass for leaving me again." She wrapped her arms under his shoulders, taking refuge in him, his strength, his warmth. "Everything in my life went to hell in one night, but losing the community center wasn't the worst of it. It was losing you all over again."

"Didn't you know I'd be back? I'd do whatever it took to convince you we belong together." He placed her left hand on his chest. "We've always belonged together."

Billy's heartbeat thundered beneath her palm. She gazed into his eyes, wondering how she'd ever doubted this man's feelings for her.

"Marry me. Right now. The courthouse is open until five."

"Yes, I'll marry you, but not today." She skimmed her hands along the ridge of his pecs. Her future husband had the most remarkable body, but it wasn't nearly as remarkable as his heart.

"Why not?"

"I have a job interview in an hour."

He frowned. "Already? With who?"

"The Patnoe family. They own the land beneath the rubble of the community center. Seems Jim White Feather showed them the tape you made and my passion for keeping the center there. They were so impressed they've vowed to rebuild as soon as possible. They want me to run it. Of course, I'd planned on turning them down."

"Why?"

"Because I was headed to the Windy City."

It was his turn to be shocked. "You'd have left all this behind for me?"

"Without question. But now it seems I have the best of both worlds."

Billy kissed her again, slowly, sweetly, with love. "Me, too." His mouth wandered down her throat. "I missed you, baby. Let me show you how much. What do you say we go inside?"

"Mmm." She arched her neck, giving him full access to all the good spots. "I say what's your hurry? We've got all the time in the world."

He groaned. "I deserved that."

"I know." Eden whispered, "But think about all of the delicious ways you can make it up to me. I'm thinking it'll take hours."

"Wrong. I'm thinking it'll take years." Billy hoisted her over his shoulder and barreled up the steps, amidst her shrieks of laughter.

"Well, then. We'd best get started right away."

Also by LORELEI JAMES

Rough Riders Legacy Series

UNBREAK MY HEART

Rough Riders Series

LONG HARD RIDE
RODE HARD
COWGIRL UP AND RIDE
TIED UP, TIED DOWN
ROUGH, RAW AND READY
STRONG SILENT TYPE (novella)
BRANDED AS TROUBLE
SHOULDA BEEN A COWBOY
ALL JACKED UP
RAISING KANE
SLOW RIDE (free short story)
COWGIRLS DON'T CRY
CHASIN' EIGHT
COWBOY CASANOVA
KISSIN' TELL
GONE COUNTRY
SHORT RIDES (anthology)
REDNECK ROMEO
COWBOY TAKE ME AWAY
LONG TIME GONE (novella)

Need You Series

WHAT YOU NEED
JUST WHAT I NEEDED
ALL YOU NEED (April 2017)

Blacktop Cowboys® Series

CORRALLED
SADDLED AND SPURRED
WRANGLED AND TANGLED
ONE NIGHT RODEO
TURN AND BURN
HILLBILLY ROCKSTAR
ROPED IN (novella)
STRIPPED DOWN (novella)
WRAPPED AND STRAPPED
STRUNG UP (novella)
HANG TOUGH (Nov 1 2016)

Mastered Series

BOUND
UNWOUND
SCHOOLED (digital only novella)
UNRAVELED
CAGED

Single Title Novels

DIRTY DEEDS

Single Title Novellas

LOST IN YOU (short novella)
WICKED GARDEN
BALLROOM BLITZ (Two to Tango anthology)
MISTRESS CHRISTMAS (Wild West Boys)
MISS FIRECRACKER (Wild West Boys)